Never Saw Me Coming

A Psychological Thriller

TANISHA STEWART

Table of Contents

Dear Reader,

Welcome to the second installment of The Quiet Ones series. I've always wanted to write a psychological thriller, but I was searching for a source of inspiration. It finally came when Ebony Evans, founder of the EyeCU Reading & Chatting group on Facebook presented a group of authors with a challenge that she calls Freestyle Fridays.

In the challenge, the authors were given a theme and a set of pictures and told to let their creative juices flow. From this challenge, Shatina's story was born. You met Shatina in Should Have Thought Twice, but the plot gets thicker in Never Saw Me Coming.

Buckle up and enjoy the ride. When you finish, I would love it if you could leave a rating or review. Happy reading!

Tanisha Stewart

Never Saw Me Coming

A Psychological Thriller

Chapter 1

Max and Shatina shared awkward glances. The room remained silent for a few moments, and Sam couldn't help but smirk at the dumbfounded looks on their faces. *This is gold,* she thought. She had them right where she wanted them. Sam poked at Max for good measure.

"Cat got your tongue?" she chuckled, then began pacing the floor.

"I don't get it," Shatina said. "How are you…what are you doing here?"

Sam pursed her lips at Shatina in a mocking fashion. "Oh, poor baby! You had no idea…" Then she smirked at Max again.

Max's tongue became unstuck from the roof of his mouth. "Sam, this isn't funny, seriously. Why are you doing this?"

Sam spun in a circle, she was so excited. "Why would I?" she repeated. "The question is, why wouldn't I? You started it."

"Started what?" Shatina looked back and forth between Sam and Max. She focused on Max. "Max, what is she talking about?"

Max's face reddened, and satisfaction swarmed in Sam's belly. He was caught. Now he had to come clean to his precious, perfect Shatina. For the life of her, Sam couldn't see what he saw in that girl, never mind that ditzy Chelsea character. Yeah, Shatina and Chelsea were cute, but Sam was sexy.

"Shatina..." Max stammered.

"Oh, come out with it!" Sam cut in. "You weren't afraid when you went after Brighton. Where's all this apprehension coming from?"

Max remained silent, so Shatina looked to Sam for answers. "How do you know Brighton Miller?"

Sam crossed her arms and pursed her lips again, this time with attitude, and cocked her head to the side.

"He's my man."

***

Max's ears grew hot after his ex-girlfriend's revelation. He knew he had done it now. He should have known Sam would catch on to him like she had last time. She was always smarter than he was. He was such an idiot.

"Shatina..." he repeated, trying to find the right words to explain.

Shatina appeared as if she was catching on. Max couldn't take the look in her eyes. "Let me get this straight. Brighton Miller is dating Sam, your ex."

Max nodded, wanting to sink into the floor as he faced his impending doom. Her next question struck him in the chest. "Is that why you were after him?"

Shatina was staring at him like she hoped his answer wasn't yes, but Max didn't want to lie to her. If there was any chance to salvage what they shared, he had to come clean.

"Yes, but it's not what you think."

Shatina's nostrils flared as she spoke her next words. "You mean to tell me, you had me risking my life to go after a politician, all because he stole your girlfriend?"

***

Shatina felt like she should have known. There was no way her and Max would have ever worked, but to think that she was involved in this entire debacle due to a silly love triangle? "This is ridiculous! I want out." She walked toward the door, but Sam held her hand up.

"Sorry, 'Tina, can't let you do that."

Shatina raised her eyebrows at Sam. "Excuse me?"

"I can't let you leave."

"You don't have to let me do anything." Shatina kept walking, but Sam's next words gave her pause.

"Sure, I can't physically stop you, or I won't at least, but just know if you leave, this recording gets leaked." Sam was holding up her cell phone with the screen facing Shatina. Shatina could see an image of herself on the screen, standing over Rodney's body with the gun she shot him with.

There was no way out. She was trapped, yet again, with not just one person who didn't have her best interest in mind, but three.

If Brighton got out of prison and Sam told him what Shatina and Max had done, they were in big trouble. If Shatina walked out, Sam would send the video of her shooting Rodney to the police. She glared at Max. This was all his fault.

"Shatina, I'm sorry," he said, and she believed him, but it didn't matter.

Shatina turned her stony expression to Sam. "What do you want us to do?"

Chapter 2

ax felt like the scum of the earth. Shatina barely looked at him on the way back to her apartment. He knew she'd only ridden home with him to keep her whereabouts inconspicuous. She didn't want to order an Uber from their meeting location in case anything got traced back to the police.

He wanted to say something, anything that would make the situation better, but his mind drew a blank.

When they pulled up to Shatina's apartment, she rushed out and slammed the passenger side door without looking back at Max.

He had to find a way to make this right.

Max turned down a side street, then kept going straight for what felt like ages. At some point, he ended up on a highway, taking a random exit to nowhere in particular. He needed to clear his mind. The problem was, he couldn't get his mind off Sam or Shatina. How could he be so stupid? Going after one exes' boyfriend for revenge, while trying to kindle something with a separate love interest, while he was in a relationship with yet another woman? His actions were reprehensible at best.

He should have never made a move on Shatina, especially with her still grieving over Seth. He'd taken advantage of her.

And Chelsea had been nothing but good to him during their time together. She helped him with his business, checked up on him to make sure he was okay, and bent over backward to be the best woman she could be. What did Max do? Take her for granted.

"Maybe this is why I could never get a girl. Maybe I wasn't meant to…" He allowed that thought to linger.

After two hours of driving, Max arrived at his apartment. He wanted nothing more than to take a long shower and contemplate his life's decisions before going to bed.

Unfortunately, it looked like Chelsea had other plans. She was sitting in her car outside his apartment. Who knew how long she'd been there.

"Hey," he said as he approached her driver's side window. "What are you doing here?"

***

Sam felt like a total boss. She gloated the entire way to her destination, replaying her last words to Shatina and Max in her mind. *I'll be in touch,* she'd said, when Shatina asked what Sam wanted her and Max to do to keep her mouth shut. Then she whirled around and sauntered out of the building, her playlist blasting as she sped away in her jeep.

Sam could only imagine the conversation Max and Shatina had after she left. "I wish I would have rigged the place with cameras."

A phone call from her father interrupted Sam's thoughts. She hit the Ignore button without hesitation, then waited for the voice message to come through. This was the third time her father had called this week, and he left a voice message each time.

Sam hadn't returned his calls and didn't plan to. Her expression darkened as she thought about why, but she refused to dwell on him. Her father didn't deserve an inch of her mental capacity.

Once her phone displayed the notification for the voice message, Sam played it with a frown, then deleted it, as she had the others.

"Oh, you want to talk to me, huh?" she mocked. "You should have thought about that before you did what you did."

***

Shatina contemplated her options. Should she let Sam dictate her life for God knew how long, or should she come clean and go to the police? She envisioned both scenarios. If she went to the police, she would likely end up in prison, regardless of her assertions that she hadn't meant for Rodney to end up dead.

You weren't the one who made the fatal shot though... the voice said.

"I wasn't, but..."

But what? It's plain as that, girl. Don't let those idiots get you wrapped up again. You see what happened last time.

Shatina could hardly forget. Max tormented her for months and disappeared, then when she thought she was done with him, he reared his ugly head again. Ironically, it was Sam who'd been Shatina's saving grace in that situation. If Sam hadn't insinuated that Max forced Shatina into helping him kidnap and murder her, Shatina would have been up the creek without a paddle. In a weird way,

Shatina contemplated whether she owed Sam for throwing out the life raft.

What could she possibly want you to do? Seth's voice asked.

Shatina froze. She was hearing it again. Seth's voice came to her from time to time, but she thought she'd heard the last of it. Apparently not.

"Seth, I'm so sorry…" Shatina stared at the background screen on her cell phone. There was a smiling selfie of her and Seth, back when things were simple. When life was good. No time to dwell on that now. Shatina had decisions to make.

The photo of her and Seth grew darker then the screen went black.

Shatina unlocked the phone again and dialed 911. As soon as her finger hit the Call button, a call from Shatara came in and Shatina accidentally answered it instead.

"Hello?" Shatina was startled by her sister's impeccable timing.

"Hey Shatina. I'm outside."

Shatina's head whipped toward her front door as if she could see through it. "You're outside? Outside for what?" She didn't have time for this right now. Shatara had no idea about everything that had been going on since what happened to Seth. Shatina didn't have the words to explain.

"I need to talk to you. Open up."

Shatina felt stuck. She stared between her phone and the door. Should she open it, or tell her sister to go away?

If she told her to go away, Shatara would likely come back with Tyonne, Tamika, and her parents, like she did last time. Shatina didn't want to deal with the drama.

That's nowhere near the level of drama you'll face in prison, the voice said.

"Shatina?" Shatara said through the phone.

Shatina rolled her eyes. "I'm coming."

She pressed the End button and opened her door.

Chapter 3

Max stepped back from Chelsea's car as she exited the driver's seat. "Chelsea, what are you doing here?" he repeated. She sighed and Max's heart dropped. Chelsea was nowhere near her usual cheerful self, and Max knew he had a part to play in that. Her hair was slightly frayed, and she was wearing a dingy white tee with cutoff shorts and flip flops. Her nails were chipped, something she always complained about during their time together. Whenever she would notice even the slightest damage, Chelsea would immediately get her whole manicure redone. What had he done to her?

"Max, you really never felt anything for me, did you?" She spoke in a sullen tone.

He wished he could give her a better answer, but if he was serious about turning over a new leaf, Max had to come clean. "Chelsea, it's not that I never cared…"

"I didn't ask if you never cared!" she spat, her red-rimmed eyes blazing into his. "I asked if you had feelings for me. There's a difference, and you know it."

Max fell silent. He didn't want to have this conversation.

A tear slid down Chelsea's cheek, but she held her head high and squared her shoulders. "That's fine," she said.

"Your body language says it all. You were never worth my time. I did everything I could for you, and you never saw my value. That's okay though. A better man will."

With those words, Chelsea got into her car. She was turning the key in the ignition when Max snapped out of it and approached her partially opened driver's side window. "Chelsea, listen. You're right. You are worth more. I sincerely hope you find the right guy because you are a great woman. You deserve better than me."

Chelsea rolled her eyes. "Whatever, Max. I'm over it. Goodbye."

She drove off, and Max felt better and worse at the same time.

***

Shatina and her sister gave each other once overs. It was ironic that once Shatina gained confidence, she and Shatara acted more like identical twins than fraternal. That was until Shatara ruined their bond with betrayal.

"Listen sis," Shatara said, gesturing as if she was trying to find her words while she was saying them. "I wanted to apologize for telling Mom and them about the voice."

Shatina scoffed. "Oh, now you want to apologize? You shouldn't have to, Shatara. You swore you would never tell a soul, and now I can't trust you."

Shatara reeled as if she'd been slapped in the face. "Shatina, I'm sorry."

"Whatever, get out of my apartment." Shatina strode to her front door for emphasis, but Shatara's demeanor changed.

She shook her head. "No."

"What do you mean, no?"

"No, Shatina. You've been pushing people away. Like I said, I apologize for what I did, but you know I only did it because I was worried about you. We all are. You can't just..."

"Shatara, I don't want to talk about this right now!" Shatina's voice thundered, and Shatara was taken aback by the suddenness of her outburst. "All of you need to leave me alone. I answer your calls and text messages, and that should be enough. None of you know what I'm going through. None of you understand, and you never will." Shatina almost said, *you never did*, but she didn't want to hurt her sister. She and Shatara shared a sincere heart to heart when Shatara first found out about the voice. Shatina didn't want to downplay that moment.

Now Shatara's eyes were filling with tears. "Shatina, how are we gonna understand if you don't let us in? Come on, girl. I'm your twin."

Shatina's lower lip trembled. She felt every word her sister was saying, but she knew she couldn't tell her everything. There was too much risk. What had she gotten herself into? This was the type of relationship she always wanted with her sister, but she couldn't have it because of all that was going on.

Still, she had to let her sister know she would be okay, or at least she hoped so. "Shatara, we're good. I'm sorry. I've just been so messed up over Seth. I know you're trying to help."

Shatara dropped her tough exterior as her facial expression melted. "Then let me in. I'm right here, sis. Our bond shouldn't break because of this. I know I wasn't always the best sister, and I really am sorry if you feel like I betrayed you, but I love you. You're the only sister I have."

They stared at each other for a few more moments. Shatina wanted to tell her sister everything, but she knew she couldn't. "I love you too, Tara. I mean that."

*****

Shatina had to go to work the next day, and her mind swirled with thoughts of Shatara, Max, and Sam. She kept asking herself how she got in this situation, until the voice halted her tracks.

Revenge, it said.

The voice was right. All of this, from the beginning, had started because of Shatina's thirst for revenge. She wanted revenge on the kids at school who bullied her, so she got it. She wanted revenge on her sister Shatara for stealing her boyfriend, so she got it. Her eyes welled up as she thought of how she wanted revenge on Seth's murderer, and she got it. Each of her actions had grown deeper and deeper without Shatina realizing it. She went from pulling pranks and messing with cars to what could be perceived as attempted murder, and then she'd finally killed someone.

Hold your horses. Remember, you didn't pull the final trigger.

True enough, Brighton had done it, but...

No, that's it. Brighton did it, not you. And you only shot Rodney to stop him from killing Max.

For once, the voice was trying to comfort her. It was right. Shatina had never held a gun until that moment, and she did only shoot Rodney as a split decision. He was going to kill Max, and she stopped him. Even if she and Max would have called an ambulance, Rodney would still be dead because of Brighton Miller. The weight of the situation was now hitting differently. The right man was behind bars. Shatina didn't deserve to go to prison.

A sense of peace overcame Shatina, and she was grateful for it, though she knew it wouldn't last. She still had to do whatever Sam wanted, and who knew what she had up her sleeve?

***

Sam decided on a date with Dallas. She hadn't seen him in a while. Brighton was in prison, and Martell wasn't back from vacation yet, so her most boring prospect would have to do. She examined the new design she'd painted onto her nails with expert precision. She blew her nails first, then placed them under her ultraviolet lights and fan so they could dry properly.

Manicures and pedicures were the only things Sam did for herself. She was rather good at them too. "Hm. Maybe I could open a salon." She thought about it for a moment, then shook her head. There was no point in opening a business if she would never be there. Sam was much too busy to trouble herself with a nine to five, or even more if she ran the nail salon all by herself.

"I could get other people to run it for me though, and then just show up when I feel like it." Her mind danced into a daydream, envisioning herself as an African American version of Meryl Streep in *The Devil Wears Prada*. "But of course, I'm nowhere near the devil though. I only apply pressure to those who slight me." Sam smirked, then checked her nails again. They were perfect, as usual. Sam popped her lips. She knew just the right dress to wear for Dallas tonight. He would be begging to take it off her before the night was over. They might not even make it past their appetizers.

Sam bounced over to her huge walk in closet, thankful for the peace and solace having her own home provided.

She could walk around naked, she could rent out rooms, she could... Her phone buzzed on her fluffy pink pillow that was sitting in the middle of her bed. Sam snatched it up to see who texted her and smiled. It was Dallas.

"Thirsty, are we?" she mused, then swiped the screen to see what he'd said.

Wear that little thing I like.

Sam blushed at the winking emoji he'd sent with the message, then responded with a risque response to match his energy. That was one thing about Dallas. His conversation might bore her to death, but his bedroom skills made up for it.

Sam laid out her little black dress and heels, then decided on a lace thong. She was going braless, which was sure to have Dallas salivating.

She took a long hot shower and washed her hair. A visualization of the perfect style hit her as she wrapped her head first, then her body in a towel and headed back into her bedroom. Sam hummed as she entered the bedroom, then shrieked and jumped back.

"Dad! How did you get in my house?"

Chapter 4

Fall semester was starting soon. Shatina was hardly excited. She signed up for four classes originally but added another to give herself a heavy distraction. There was a new neuroscience course being offered, and Shatina thought it would fit well with her Dark Psychology and Cognitive Psychology courses. She was also taking biology and statistics. At first she was satisfied with her decision, then she worried she was doing too much. Her finger hovered over the Unenroll button for the Dark Psychology course. She'd originally signed up for it with Seth, who told her it would be interesting to learn about the sinister side of human nature and the powers of manipulation. It was ironic that Seth picked the course rather than Shatina. Seth carried himself like an angel, always smiling and joking and tutoring classmates and volunteering for his community. The same community where he was murdered.

Shatina focused back on her screen.

Maybe Seth wanted to take the course because he saw the darkness in you, the voice said. *Maybe he knew something was off. Maybe he sensed that one day you would have it in you to kill a man.*

"Ugh, whose side are you on?" Shatina groaned.

The voice didn't respond.

Maybe next semester she should take a course related to psychiatry. The university sometimes allowed undergraduate students to enroll in graduate level courses if they held a high GPA and the instructor allowed them. Shatina's original goal was to pursue a career as a clinical psychologist. She was sure she could convince her advisor to...

She clicked on the school's page for the Dark Psychology course. The first thing she noticed was that the instructor didn't have his full name listed. While other professor's names were listed as *Dr.* this or that, his name was listed as *Ted*. Assuming it was a man. Shatina wracked her brain for female names which could be shortened to Ted. None that she could think of.

Ted also didn't have a headshot, or a long description of his accomplishments and publications listed on his faculty profile. His photo was a red question mark with a black background. Shatina wrinkled her nose. "The dean let him get away with this?"

Ted's credentials were listed as *pending*.

"Is he new?" Shatina was intrigued by this man already. Why was he purposefully standing out?

She was definitely not dropping his class now.

Her fingers tapped the keys to get to ratemyprofessor.com. She didn't have much to go on, since Ted only listed his first name, but she found him. He had a controversial profile to say the least. Some students complained about him being a total jerk, while others hailed him as the most brilliant professor they ever encountered.

Shatina wasn't sure what to think. "Am I gonna like this guy?"

She went back to the school's website and stared at the Unenroll button again.

Take the course, Seth's voice said, or maybe it was Shatina's desperation speaking. Anything that would help her hold onto a piece of Seth would do. She clicked out of the website, her final decision made.

Hopefully Ted wasn't too much of a jerk, like some had said.

***

Sam applied burgundy lipstick in front of her vanity mirror. Perfect. She batted her lashes for more effect, then puckered before switching the light off.

Her father, Dexter, had almost ruined the night with his appearance, but she had gotten him to leave, thankfully.

"Samantha," he said. "You can't avoid me forever. Let's talk about this."

"Talk about what, Dad?" she shot back. "You already said your piece, and I said mine."

Dexter raised his hand to reach out to her, then let it rest at his side. "I already told you I'm sorry. If you can't accept my apology…"

"You've been sorry all my life!" Sam's pressure was raising, she knew it. "All you've been is sorry, Dad. Ever since the day I was born. Since I was a child. Remember?"

Dexter tried again. "Samantha…"

"It's Sam."

"Sam…"

"Just leave."

Dexter's features hardened. "No, I'm not leaving until we settle this."

18

Sam flipped her hand at him. "There's nothing to settle. You are who you are. You're not going to change, so there's no point in me holding out hope for the better."

Those words had wounded Dexter, Sam could tell, but she didn't care. Served him right, for what he had done.

Dexter had left shortly after that, and Sam was unbothered. She continued getting ready, pampering herself in preparation for her date with Dallas.

"He better not bore me to tears over dinner, or I'll halt it after appetizers myself." Sam's eyes blurred, then she realized she was crying.

"Oh no you don't!" she scolded herself. "Dexter doesn't deserve your emotions." Dexter had hurt her deeply every time she let her guard down to give him a chance to prove himself, but Sam refused to dwell on him any further.

She was focused on Dallas now. He would be her distraction for tonight, and possibly the next week, until Martell's flight came in.

Sam freshened up her face then headed out the door.

***

Max called Shatina for the third time, but just like all the others, it rang until it went to voicemail. He sighed, then flipped his phone onto the kitchen table.

The cold glass of Jack Daniels was numbing his hand, but Max didn't care. He took another sip, a cube of ice dropping out onto his neck, then getting caught in his collar. Max flicked the ice cube to the floor, then downed the rest of the glass, refilling it afterward with the bottle from the table. His life was in shambles.

Shatina wasn't talking to him, Sam was up to God knew what, and he'd broken Chelsea's heart.

He had no one to call, no one to talk to about his troubles. His relationship with his parents and their son was far from amicable, and Max had no friends.

Just then, a text buzzed through on his phone. *Where you been at, man?*

Max sighed. It was one of his clients, asking for pills. He hadn't sold anything since Rodney's murder. If he did go back to his illicit activities, it wouldn't be long before he ran out. Rodney was his main supplier. Max knew other guys, but he wasn't sure if he wanted to get wrapped up any further. He already had a potential murder case on his back, depending on what Sam had up her sleeve for him and Shatina. If she requested something too outlandish, Max would pretend like he was going along with it, then block her from his phone and turn himself in.

He was prepared to take the fall for everything, excluding Shatina from responsibility. Max knew how to deal with police. They would likely believe his story anyway, especially with his prior run ins, not to mention the fact that he had been expelled from his college for the same type of behavior.

Max was a failure all around. Maybe prison was his lot in life.

His phone buzzed again, and Max sucked his teeth. He picked it up to tell the person to find another dealer, then decided against it. He needed to get out of this apartment anyway, and he was in a reckless mood. He would take all the pills he had with him. If he was caught by the cops, so what? One more charge to add to the list. That would probably thoroughly convince them of his guilt in Rodney's murder. He was already a drug dealer, why not a killer?

Max cringed at the thoughts of what awaited him inside the walls of whatever facility he would be sent to, but he shrugged it off.

He texted the client, Gerard, back to let him know he was on the way.

Max sped the whole way there, then screeched to a stop in the convenience store parking lot where Gerard said to meet him.

Just his luck, there were no cops in sight. Any other time and he would have been pulled over for erratic driving behavior. Unfortunately, not tonight.

Gerard came out of the store immediately. "Long time no see!" He shot Max a crooked smile that wasn't returned. "What's good with you, man?"

Max shook his head. "Nothing, man, but listen. I'm running low so you may need to find someone new soon."

Gerard looked taken aback. "What? Why, man. You got the best stuff!"

Max didn't bother to answer. He held the tube of pills out in plain sight, and Gerard snatched them and stuffed them in his pocket, giving him a strange look in response.

"You sure you good man?" His eyes narrowed.

Max shrugged, ready for this conversation to be over. "That's what I said."

Gerard sighed. "Alright." He handed Max the money. "How much you got left?" He eyed the black duffel bag that Max had taken the tube of pills out of, which was openly displayed in the passenger's seat. Gerard glanced over at some other guys who were posted up in front of the store, and Max put two and two together. He wasn't getting robbed tonight.

"Chill, just hit me up when you need more. I'll let you know when I'm done for good."

Max peeled out of the parking lot before Gerard had a chance to make any other moves.

22

Chapter 5

Sam pulled up to Melody's, the five star restaurant her and Dallas were having dinner at. She allowed the valet to take her jeep, pretending not to notice his ogling eyes, then made her way into the lobby.

Dallas better not be late.

No sooner than she had the thought, Dallas pulled up outside. Sam watched him joke with the valet, then dap him up before he entered the lobby with a smile.

Sam had to admit, Dallas had a sexy smile. His goatee was freshly groomed, and his muscular frame filled out his suit.

He was wearing non prescription Gucci glasses with black frames.

"Don't you look distinguished?" Sam flirted, and Dallas blushed.

"Only the best for my lady."

Her eyebrow raised at that comment, but Sam didn't bother to correct him. Why not let him think she was his for the night? Martell wasn't due back yet anyway, plus Brighton was still locked up. Who knew how long that would last? Her and Dallas would probably be seeing more of each other than usual until the situation blew over.

Dallas placed his hand on the small of her back as they approached the hostess, and Sam knew it was because he wanted to touch her bare skin. She smirked. The backless dress did it every time, not that it left much else to the imagination. It was a slutty and classy dress, all at the same time, with a plunging neckline in the front, and the length barely passed her thighs. *Guess I'll be his little whore tonight.* Sam's smirk deepened as devilish thoughts danced through her mind.

Dallas seemed to catch her drift. He'd been staring at her nipples through her dress, but he looked away and cleared his throat when she caught his eye. From the half-smile that played across his lips, Sam knew he had the same things on his mind that she did.

The hostess led them to their table, introduced their waitress, then moved on.

Sam perused the menu, her eyes scanning the more expensive items. The prices weren't listed, but she had been to this place before with Martell and knew just how high they could go.

"Should we start with a bottle of Chardonnay," she was asking, but before Sam could finish her sentence, another woman pulled up a chair and plopped down at the table.

Dallas' face reddened and he stumbled over his words. "Marcia…I…didn't you have to work tonight?"

Sam let her menu fall to the floor. "Who are you?" She eyed the woman who had the audacity to intercept her dinner date.

Marcia was dressed to kill with a stunning red dress and Red Bottom heels to match, but she was still no match for Sam. Still, she gave Sam a cocky look as she spoke. "I'm Dallas' woman, and you are?"

***

Shatina please. We need to talk. Max had sent the text message an hour ago, but Shatina hadn't responded. She knew she had to deal with him eventually, but she didn't feel up to it at the moment.

Her phone buzzed with another text. She lazily picked it up, expecting another pleading request, but the color drained from her face when she saw what Max had written.

I understand you don't want to talk to me. I don't blame you. Outside the police station now. I'll take the full blame. Goodbye.

She called him immediately.

"Hello?" he answered in a numb tone.

"Max, what are you doing?" she hissed. "Are you really at the police station?"

He was silent for a moment. "Yes."

"Why would you go there? Brighton already turned himself in. We should just let it play out. Remember, he did that to Rodney, not us."

His tone was hollow. "I don't want to hurt anyone anymore."

When she heard the slur in his pronunciation, Shatina put two and two together. "Max, stay in your car. I'm on my way."

"Okay."

She arrived less than fifteen minutes later, rolling down her passenger side window and signaling for Max to do the same with his driver's side. His eyes were bloodshot, and Shatina's suspicions were confirmed. He was drunk.

"We gotta get you home," she said, as soon as his window slid down.

"You don't think I should go in there?" he pointed at the building for emphasis.

"No, Max, you shouldn't. Follow me."

"Shatina…"

"Follow me!" she demanded, then pulled out of her space, heading toward the exit. Thankfully Max followed, and not a moment too soon, because there was an officer exiting the building. The officer stared at Max's car as he exited the lot.

"They were probably about to start questioning him," Shatina said, then she thought about it. Her anxiety rose as she considered the possibility that Max had just outed them. Why go to the police station? What if they looked at the cameras and ran his plates? What if they put two and two together? What if…

"No." Shatina shook her head. "They have no idea why Max was outside, and they're not going to look into it. Why would they? He didn't do anything suspicious."

She calmed herself as she turned down Max's street, contemplating whether she should stay the night.

Max obviously couldn't be left to his own devices.

They exited their vehicles and went inside.

***

Max's mind was swimming. He had finished the bottle of Jack Daniels before heading to the police station. It was a wonder he made it all the way there and back in one piece.

His eyelids were growing heavier as each moment passed.

"Max?" Shatina was saying. She was standing over him in front of the couch, but Max was too tired to engage. He was down for the count before she could say another word.

When he woke up the next morning, Shatina was still there.

Max wasn't sure if that was a good thing or a bad thing, until Shatina set up a TV tray in front of him, then thrust a cup of coffee and a plate of scrambled eggs, bacon, and blueberry waffles in front of him. "Eat." She grunted, but Max knew from her kind gesture that she still cared about him.

He hoped that meant there was a chance to make things right.

Chapter 6

Sam could not believe Dallas' gall. True enough, she had a few men she was seeing, but for him to lie to her when she asked if he was with anyone? It was on. Last night had ended with Dallas' girlfriend pouring a drink over his head, but Sam knew from the look in her eyes they would be back together before the end of the week.

Dallas and Sam were through. A man had one time to lie to Sam before she not only cut him off, but he felt her wrath. Martell had never lied to her, but Max and Brighton both had, and she made them pay. Dallas would soon learn who not to play with.

A call from a correctional facility came through on her cell phone while Sam was in the middle of plotting her revenge on Dallas. "Saved by the bell," she said, and answered.

"Hello?"

It was Brighton. "Hey baby." The idiot sounded so forlorn, Sam almost felt sorry for him.

"What do you want, Brighton?" Sam rolled her eyes while she inspected the design on her pointer finger. She thought she saw a crack in it.

"Sam, I need to see you."

That was a crack. This had to be fixed immediately. "For what? Shouldn't you have been bailed out by now?"

"Why are you acting like this? Aren't you worried about me?"

Not really, she almost said, but that would have been too harsh. "Of course I'm worried, Brighton, but realistically, what can I do for you? You've gotten yourself in a sticky situation." Sam glanced around her room to find her gel polish. Where had she left it?

"I need you to talk to McConnell." His tone was direct, and Sam knew exactly what Brighton was saying. McConnell was his lawyer. Brighton wanted her to look over whatever dirt McConnell said they had on him and help him get out of it.

Sam played dumb, pausing her search for a moment to pay attention to Brighton. "Talk to McConnell? Brighton, I'm not sure how me talking to him will help your cause. What am I supposed to do? I'm not a lawyer."

Brighton sighed, indicating he was not trying to play Sam's game today. "Sam, please just call the man?"

The automated voice cut in telling them they had a minute left to speak. Sam told Brighton she would reach out in a few days, then hung up the phone.

Of course, she not only knew everything McConnell had for Brighton as far as evidence, she knew who was responsible for him being locked up in the first place. Sam wasn't going to lift a finger to help until she was good and ready. If that time ever came.

Brighton was a cheater, after all. She found out that minor detail right when she was about to have her contact hack into Max's computer to delete the footage from the night of Rodney's murder.

When she saw pictures of the skank Brighton was cheating with, Sam left Shatina and Max's electronic devices alone.

"Oops," she said with a shrug, then grabbed her gel polish from the shelf on her vanity set.

***

Max and Shatina ate in silence before Max broke the ice. "Thanks for last night."

Shatina stared straight ahead at the blank TV screen. "Yup."

"You didn't have to come out and get me like that. I appreciate you."

"I heard when you said it the first time." Her expression was stony. This wasn't going to be easy.

"Shatina, what can I do to make this right?"

She snorted. "Do you know anywhere we can rent a time machine?"

That one hurt. Max heard her message loud and clear. She was saying the only way to make it right was if they had never met one another.

Max stood and picked his empty plate and cup up off the tray. He reached his hand out to Shatina and she handed hers to him too. At least she was being cordial.

Max took his time in the kitchen, washing the dishes and contemplating his next move. He had to find a way to get through to her. They couldn't go on like this, not with everything that had happened over the last month or so. They had gone from enemies, to *associates*, as Shatina had previously joked, to the possibility of something more, before everything got ruined.

Max placed the last dish in the rack, then walked back toward the living room. He was going to try again.

Unfortunately, he lost his chance. Shatina was gone.

He was so in the zone while he was washing dishes he didn't realize she had walked out of his apartment. He peeked out the blinds in the living room, and her car was gone too. Max's shoulders slumped, but he fought to remain encouraged. If she was cordial enough to share a meal with him, there was still a chance they could work it out. He was going to do everything in his power to make things right again.

***

Shatina felt bad for being mean to Max, then walking out on him while he was in the kitchen, but another part of her didn't care. If Max hadn't been such a liar and a sneak, they wouldn't be in the situation they were in.

To think, she had believed she was falling for him. When they kissed that night before Sam showed her face, Shatina was seriously considering what life would be like with Max. They seemed to fit, in a weird way. Now she didn't know what to think.

How could he possibly be serious about her, when his whole reason for them working together was to get back at his ex-girlfriend's new boyfriend?

"I guess I shouldn't be surprised," Shatina said as she put her blinker on to turn down her street. "He used Chelsea the same way he used me."

Max had revealed how Chelsea helped him build his stalker business, designing his website and printing his business cards. If he could dog out a woman like that, what made Shatina think she was special?

"Ew." She scrunched up her face. "Why would I want Max to think I'm special anyway?"

Shatina pressed the button for her contacts on the dashboard. She was about to give Max a piece of her mind, since he was so desperate for her conversation, but she stopped herself. She remembered how humiliated she felt for Chelsea when she was blowing up Max's phone back to back. Granted, it was based on faulty reasoning because Max wasn't cheating with Shatina, but still. As Shatina had stared at Max's phone lighting up for half the night while he slept like a baby, she told herself she could never. Now here she was, about to call the same man for a similar reason.

"Not today."

She pulled up to her apartment, staring at the front door for a long time before shutting her car off to go in. She hated being alone, but that was exactly how she felt these days.

"Sam needs to hurry up and tell us what she wants, so I can move on with my life."

Shatina entered her apartment, kicking off her shoes and heading toward her bedroom to change into something more comfortable.

Chapter 7

Max opened his eyes and stretched, then almost pissed himself when his arm touched a body that was lying next to him.

"Sam! What the hell are you doing here?" He jerked away out of pure instinct.

Sam appeared to be unbothered. She was laying under his covers next to him, but when she scooted up into a sitting position and lowered the blanket to her lap, he saw that she was dressed in a lavender bra and panty set. She smiled as his eyes took in her appearance, then he looked away.

"What are you doing here?" he asked again, this time in a lower tone.

"I came to see you!"

Sam's bright and sunny demeanor was too much for Max. "How did you get into my apartment?"

"Your kitchen window was unlocked." She shrugged as if it was no big deal.

What is with these women breaking into my apartment? Max was puzzled, but decided to focus on the more pressing matter. "Why do you feel you need to see me? And couldn't you have called first, instead of breaking in and climbing into my bed practically naked?"

She shot him a devilish smirk. "It's nothing you haven't seen before."

Max remembered all too well what Sam's body looked and felt like, but he preferred not to let those thoughts linger. He stood to go to the bathroom.

"Come on. Get your clothes on. This isn't funny."

As he strode toward the door, Sam giggled.

"Come on, no need to be upset. It's not like you have a girlfriend anymore. Shatina ruined that one, didn't she?"

Max whipped his head toward her. He was in his doorway when her comment reached his ears. "How did you know about that?"

Her grin didn't falter. "I have my ways."

Max sighed. "Sam, you're confusing me. The last time we spoke to each other, you cut me off and said you never wanted to see me again. Now I find out you've been keeping tabs on me the whole time? What for? And why drag Shatina into your shenanigans?"

Sam was studying him as he spoke. "Why are you so worried about Shatina?"

Max couldn't believe his ears. "Was that all you heard from what I just said?"

Sam shrugged. "It was the only relevant part."

"Why is that relevant? Again, you cut me off, not the other way around."

Sam laughed seductively. "Are you saying you still want me?"

Max scrunched his face. "No, that's not what I'm saying. I'm... Sam, get out of my house, please."

He went to the bathroom to relieve himself, then when he returned, Sam was in the process of plumping the pillows on his freshly made bed. This was bizarre. *Is she on drugs?* Her behavior was erratic to say the least. When they were together, all Sam did was complain about his lack of bedroom skills and how he was a lowlife who would never amount to anything.

Now that he'd gone after her boyfriend, she was suddenly interested?

Sam walked up to Max, still only wearing her bra and panties. He couldn't help but to be turned on by her body, but he wasn't going down that road again. He cleared his throat.

"Brighton called me," she said, and that helped him snap out of his lustful moment.

He tensed up. "And said what? Did you tell him anything?"

The corners of her lips turned up. "Nope! I didn't say a word. But I could have." Her lids lowered.

Max tried to figure out her angle. "What do you want from me, Sam?"

They stared at each other for a moment, then Sam's serious expression broke into another grin. "You and Shatina can meet me on Friday at seven, same location as last time. I'll discuss the details then." With those words, she grabbed her jeans and blouse from the floor and put them on.

"That's it? You broke into my house and spent the night just to say that?" Max didn't know what to make of Sam's recent actions.

She didn't respond to his question. She just slid her feet into her sandals and left his apartment.

***

A text buzzed through from Max while Shatina was walking back from her lunch break at work, telling her the time and location of the meeting with Sam.

Shatina rolled her eyes. She was hoping Sam would change her mind about having them help her with whatever plan she had cooked up. Hopefully it was nothing criminal.

Shatina sighed as she entered the building and ambled toward her station, then her lips curled into an involuntary smile as she saw the Ice Queen, a woman who'd harassed her a few weeks ago, come to the deli line. *I wonder if she got her car fixed?*

Memories of that day filled Shatina's mind. The woman had been so mean to her, and Shatina couldn't help but to return the favor when she saw her car in the parking lot. A quick push of a cart, and her work was done. She had never been questioned by the department store's security team or her manager, so Shatina figured she was home free. *Serves her right,* the voice said, as Shatina watched the Ice Queen torment her coworker.

Shatina washed her hands then put on gloves to resume her duties. She could tell her coworker, Mara, couldn't wait to be done with the impossible woman.

"Anything else, Ma'am?" Mara asked.

The Ice Queen turned up her nose. "That will be all." She held out her hand to take the packages of smoked turkey from Mara. Then her eyes cut to Shatina.

Shatina was caught off guard by the abruptness of the gesture. It was as if the Ice Queen was staring through her, like she knew what Shatina had done. Or maybe she was just being paranoid.

"Hmph," the woman said. "Seems someone has learned customer service skills around here."

Neither Shatina nor Mara bothered to respond as the woman walked away. Their line was filling up anyway.

***

Sam sat in the parking lot of Dallas' job. She peered through her binoculars, waiting for him to walk out any minute now. Her heart warmed with gleeful anticipation. "Come on..." she breathed, then it happened.

Dallas emerged, flanked by two security officers. His expression was sullen. Sam knew exactly why. As soon as he found the dirt, Sam instructed her contact to send it to Dallas' Human Resources manager. It was no one's fault but Dallas' own. He should have known better than to skim money off of the company's charity fund.

He fronted like he lived a lavish lifestyle to please the ladies, but Dallas was nothing more than a glorified schemer. Sam froze as she realized this seemed to be a pattern for her. Max was a schemer too, and so was Brighton, just in different ways.

Martell was legit, as far as she knew. Perhaps she should have her contact run a check on him... Just as she had the thought, Martell sent her a text. *Hey. In the baggage claim area. You here?*

Sam smirked. Martell had told her to meet him at the airport a half hour ago, but she wasn't about to sit at the pickup station twiddling her thumbs until his flight came in. No, he could wait for her.

Sorry babe! Time slipped by me. Be there in ten.

Of course, the trip was more like forty five minutes rather than ten, but who was counting? Sam laughed at Dallas' demise one last time before she headed toward the airport for a much awaited reunion with Martell.

Chapter 8

Shatina exited her job after a long day, wanting nothing more than to go home and sleep. Unfortunately, Sam had other plans. She was sitting on the hood of Shatina's car, wearing her signature smirk. Sam stood and curtsied when Shatina approached her.

"Hello my lady!"

Shatina stared at her. "Why are you here?" She wouldn't bother to ask how Sam knew where she worked. It was clear that she was either having her and Max followed, or she found some way to track them through technology. A migraine was coming on, so Shatina hoped this conversation was quick.

"Did Max tell you about our upcoming meeting?"

Shatina's eyes narrowed. "Yeah, why?"

Sam shrugged in a pompous manner. "Just wanted to make sure you knew. Max and I discussed it the other day after we spent the night together." Once she made that comment, Sam studied Shatina as if she was waiting for her to flinch.

Shatina didn't have time for this. "Was that supposed to make me jealous or something? If so, girl bye. Nobody wants Max, except you, apparently."

Sam appeared to be enjoying their back and forth. "I understand if you're intimidated, sis. I probably would be too, if the man I wanted was always around someone he had history with."

"Sam, I don't know what you think you're doing here, but this ain't it. I don't want Max. Why are you so pressed for me to compete with you anyway? If I wanted Max, I could have him, and I would never have to worry about you. Besides, do you really think blackmailing him is the way to his heart? Try a different method, sis."

Sam stared for a moment longer before she backed off. "See you Friday, Shatina."

Shatina watched as she got in her car and drove off. That was one of the weirdest interactions she ever experienced. Why was Sam trying to force her to fight for Max's affections?

Maybe she's trying to get into your head, the voice suggested.

Shatina shook it off and headed home.

***

Sam was slightly disappointed that her interaction with Shatina wasn't as hostile as she envisioned. She knew Shatina was feeling Max though, regardless of what she said. From what Chelsea told her, Shatina was always in Max's face, and he had felt the need to keep their relationship a secret until he got caught.

"Hm..." she said.

As if on cue, Chelsea sent Sam a message. *Hey girl, guess what?*

Sam directed her dashboard to respond. *What's up?*

Got a date tomorrow! He's cute too. Sending a pic now.

Sam glanced at the picture when she stopped at a light, and texted Chelsea that she approved, but she was thinking of a way to get rid of the woman. Her unintentional services were no longer needed.

Sam had found out about Chelsea when she saw her tag Max in a selfie they took together on her page. Sam waited a few days, then sent her a friend request. She joined a few groups Chelsea was in first to make it seem like they hung in mutual circles, and Chelsea bit the bait.

From that point, it was easy to crack her. All Sam had to do was leave a few friendly comments here and there and place a heart emoji on some of Chelsea's pictures, and she was in. The woman divulged a lot about her relationship with Max. Sam encouraged and prodded her for information from time to time. When Chelsea mentioned that some skank named Shatina had popped up all of a sudden, Sam's alarm bells rang. What was Max doing hanging with Shatina? Sam knew how they met, as well as why their interactions ended. She reached out to her contact for him to dig up some info, and low and behold, Max was after Brighton. That intrigued Sam, to say the least, because it proved to her that Max still wanted her. She originally planned to toy with him, but once Brighton killed Rodney, Sam decided to up the ante. Besides, Max and Shatina were the perfect people to help complete her next plan of revenge against Lacey.

Sam hoped they were smooth enough to pull it off.

***

Max was up for half the night trying to come up with a plan to get rid of Sam. He didn't like the direction this situation was headed. Sam seemed to like toying with him, and when she mentioned Brighton, it made Max believe

41

that she might sell him out to the police despite him going along with her plan.

She had sold him out before, why not again?

Granted, the first time was for good reason - he had planned to kidnap and murder her for leaving him for Brighton, and she caught onto his plan, but still.

Please tell your girlfriend to stop showing up at my job, Shatina texted, disrupting his thoughts.

Max wrinkled his nose. *What are you talking about?*

Her highness.

He sucked his teeth. *Sorry about that. She showed up at my apartment too.*

I know. She told me all about your escapades.

"Escapades?"

There was no escapade. She wasn't invited.

I bet.

Was Shatina upset with him? Max couldn't tell. She seemed to be, judging from the fact that she sounded irritated at the prospect of him and Sam messing around. He called her instead of texting a response, but she didn't answer.

That pissed him off, but he wasn't going to address it. Instead, he texted, *See you tomorrow.*

Again, she didn't respond.

Chapter 9

Sam had gone all out for the occasion, having her contact prepare three-ring binders for herself, Shatina and Max containing the details for her plan. She told them to be at the location at seven, but of course, she had to make them sweat by showing up at seven fifty-three. Sam relished at the irritated looks on their faces when she waltzed in the door of the cabin, binders wrapped in her arm.

"Let's get started, shall we?"

Shatina rolled her eyes, and Max stood with his fists clenched.

"Loosen up, will you?" Sam chuckled. "This will be fun! You two obviously enjoy completing missions together, so this should be a piece of cake." She gestured toward the wooden table and chairs for Max and Shatina to sit down. Of course, Sam assumed her position at the head of the table, where she belonged.

Shatina and Max sat across from each other. They shared a look that Sam didn't appreciate, but she wasn't going to address it at the moment.

"Ahem." Sam cleared her throat. "Here is your target." She slid a binder in each of their directions.

Shatina wrinkled her nose, staring at the binder's black cover. "Is all this necessary?"

Sam smirked. "Go ahead. Open it."

Max and Shatina opened their binders simultaneously, and the first page contained the ugliest picture of Lacey Sam could find. It was a headshot photo from a modeling agency. Sam had her contact pay the photographer for all of the worst looking photos so Sam could have options to choose from.

She watched as they both stared at the headshot with blank expressions, then looked back at her.

"Who is this?" Max asked. "I'm not killing anyone."

Sam laughed. "Silly, why would you think I'd have you do a thing like that? I'm not a murderer, darling. That's you and your girl, Shatina."

Shatina's face reddened. "No, that's your man, Brighton." She shot daggers in Sam's direction.

Sam pursed her lips. "Touché. Turn the page."

They did as she instructed, and Sam thoroughly enjoyed watching them acquiesce her every demand. The second page was another photo of Lacey, but from a further angle.

"Okay, I don't get it." The impatience in Max's tone was unmistakable. "What, is this binder full of pictures of some chick? What do you want from us, Sam?"

Sam opened her mouth to reply, but Shatina cut her off. "She wants us to steal the necklace."

Both Sam and Max were caught off guard by Shatina's assessment but for different reasons.

"What necklace?" Max asked.

"How did you know?" Sam asked.

"That's the only difference in the two photos," Shatina replied as if it was obvious. "She's wearing the same dress in both. The only difference is that she's wearing the necklace in this second photo."

Shatina turned to page three in her binder and her suspicions were confirmed. She pushed her binder toward Max. "See?"

The third page contained an up close photo of the necklace Lacey was wearing.

Max looked at Shatina's binder, then back at Sam. "Why do you want us to steal the necklace? It looks expensive, but you're not hard up for cash."

Sam was rattled by the fact that Shatina was smarter than she originally thought, but she forced herself not to let it show. "I have my reasons," she said in a cold voice. "Anyway, there's a Thanksgiving gala Lacey's family holds every year at their mansion. Your task is to…"

Shatina cut in. "Wait a minute…Thanksgiving?"

Sam smirked, happy to have regained her footing. Shatina was the one who looked flustered now. "Yes, Thanksgiving."

It was Max's turn to express his frustration. "You mean to tell me we have to have this looming over our heads for the next three months?"

Sam's smile widened. "I wouldn't explain it using that terminology, but yes, I wanted to provide ample time to prepare. This has to be done with precision, because there's no way she's keeping that necklace."

That last part came out a lot more harsh than Sam intended, but she didn't care. They were doing this, and that stupid smug look Lacey perpetually wore would be permanently erased from her features. Or at least that was what Sam envisioned.

She explained the rest of the plan, then left before Max or Shatina could ask any more questions.

***

Max wished he had never gone after Brighton. Now Sam had him and Shatina going on dummy missions. After Sam left, Max and Shatina stared at each other.

"Can you believe this?" he asked, but he was really trying to test the waters. Depending on how Shatina responded, he would know if she was still upset with him.

Shatina rolled her eyes. "You sure know how to pick them."

He couldn't tell from that response how Shatina was feeling, so he pressed further. "Listen, Shatina. I know I already apologized, but once again, I'm sorry. If I had any idea it would lead to all this, I never would have gone after Brighton, much less asked for your help."

She sighed. "It's not totally your fault. I wanted to go after Seth's killer just as much as you wanted what you wanted. We both made dumb moves, and now we both have to pay for it."

They sat in silence for a few moments.

Max cracked a joke. "Look on the bright side. At least she doesn't want us to kill anyone."

Shatina rolled her eyes again, but gave him a half smile that let him know they were on better terms.

***

Shatina wished with all her might that she could find a way to turn this all back on Sam and make her disappear for good. She didn't want the woman dead, she wanted her out of her life. Who did Sam think she was, calling shots like she was some kind of crime boss?

Her pompous attitude definitely had to go.

Thanksgiving couldn't get here quick enough, then this whole situation would hopefully be over.

But will it though? the voice said. *Brighton's case isn't over yet.*

Shatina had almost forgot. "Thanks for the reminder," she said in a sarcastic tone.

Chapter 10

It was time to start the fall semester. Shatina hadn't heard from Sam since she called the meeting with her and Max. She texted back and forth with Max a few times, but they hadn't seen each other since the meeting either.

Shatina hoped her new classes would be a welcome distraction. She felt a rush of excitement mixed with depression as she showered to prepare for her day. The excitement came because she enjoyed school. The more she learned about psychology, the more she wanted to learn. The depression set in because this would be her first semester back without Seth. Thankfully, the university hosted a large campus, but still. Because Shatina and Seth were athletes, they were well known by many students, staff, and faculty.

Shatina had somewhat lived in a bubble by taking a hiatus from her social media accounts, but now that everyone would be back on campus, she would be forced to deal with reality. Last night, she emailed her coach and told him she was no longer interested in being on the track team. He had let her skip their summer schedule due to the tragedy she'd endured, but he wasn't happy to hear she was quitting the team altogether.

Shatina, please don't do this, he'd written. *You've grown so much since joining. Everyone will be sad to see you go.*

She didn't bother to respond. Her coach didn't understand, but she wasn't about to sit there while everyone threw a pity party around her. Before she went on her social media hiatus, her teammates had blown up her page with their condolences and various pictures of themselves with Seth. Shatina couldn't take it. Most of them were genuine, but one thing Shatina could not deal with was fakes. She knew for a fact that some of the guys on the team were jealous of Seth because of his record. He was one of the best. It was unmistakable.

Shatina's mom FaceTimed her as she was heading out of her apartment to her car. She sucked her teeth, wanting badly to reject it, but she knew she couldn't. She mustered up a fake smile and answered.

"Hey."

"Hey honey. Are you headed to school?"

"Yup. About to get in the car now." Shatina hoped those words would cause her mother to end the conversation quickly. Her mom was always telling her and Shatara to never talk or text while driving, even through Bluetooth.

"Okay, well I won't hold you. I know it has to be tough going back to school."

Shatina wasn't sure how to respond to that statement. "Yup," she said, hoping she didn't come off as rude.

"I'll talk to you later. About to call Shatara now."

"Okay, talk soon." Shatina ended the call before her mother could say anything else.

Her phone buzzed with texts from Tyonne and Tamika, who Shatina had been avoiding lately. Things weren't the same between them since they graduated high school and went in separate directions for college. Tyonne and Tamika had their own lives, and Shatina had hers. Of course, they would always be connected since Tyonne was her cousin and Tamika was her best friend, but their relationships were nowhere near where they used to be. Tamika had grown close to some of the other girls at her college, and Shatina hadn't had a problem with it since she was busy with Seth. Now that he was gone, she felt awkward. She hadn't made strong friendships with anyone else at the school, though she was cool with her former teammates and roommate.

Shatina pondered whether she should try building stronger bonds with any of them, but before she could go too deeply into that thought process, Shatara texted her phone.

Hey sis. Just got off the phone with Mom. Hope everything's well with you. She sent a heart emoji along with the message.

For some reason, that warmed Shatina's heart. She didn't have to look for outside friendships, she had a whole twin sister sitting right there. Granted, Shatara was at a different school hundreds of miles away, but they could keep closer contact with each other via FaceTime and text. Shatina didn't know if it was grief over Seth or what, but for the first time in her life, she felt like she needed someone. Someone to hold onto. Someone to encourage her when the days got dark.

She was sure Shatara could be that person for her, since she was the only one outside of Max who knew some of her darkest secrets. At the same time, she couldn't tell Shatara everything that was going on. She would have to keep the whole Max/Brighton/Sam fiasco a secret, though that situation was bothering her just as much as Seth's death, if not more.

How are you going to build a bond, if you can't be real with her? the voice said.

Shatina pulled into a parking space in front of the psychology building, where three of her courses this semester would be held.

"I'll just have to figure it out." She grabbed her backpack and exited her vehicle, heading inside the building.

Chapter 11

Max felt like he didn't have anything better to do with his life, so he decided to focus on his clients until Sam came calling. Shatina was back at school. They had been texting and calling each other, but Max wasn't sure how to move forward. In his heart, he wanted to pursue something with Shatina, but every time he mustered up the courage to mention it, he lost his steam. Truth be told, he feared her rejection. Plus he wasn't entirely sure she was over Seth. No way she could be. It had been less than two months since he was murdered.

The more Max dealt with clients, the more Shatina's words that night they went after Rodney came back to him. She was eyeing his binoculars, which he had rigged to record video, audio, and pictures, and she told him he was wasting his talents.

Ever since that night, he couldn't get her words out of his mind. The only problem was, he didn't know where to start to use his talents in the right way. His drug dealing was sure to lead him behind prison walls if he ever got caught, and his other business technically wasn't criminal, but still.

"Maybe I should be a private investigator. That's sort of what I'm doing anyway." He thought about it, but wasn't sure where he should start.

How about the internet? His mind sarcastically replied. It was funny that Max knew all about the wonders of technology until it came to doing something good.

Still, once this whole situation with Sam blew over, he wanted to turn over a new leaf. He doubted any colleges would accept him after being expelled.

A community college might, he thought. He hadn't considered that option before but now it was appealing.

Instead of looking up community colleges with IT programs, Max searched news sites for updates on Brighton's case. Since it was high profile, there was some sort of update every day, but in reality, the case hadn't made much progress. All the sites Max read contained statements saying the same thing in different ways, that Brighton's lawyer was trying to gather more evidence for his case. Brighton hadn't been awarded bail because the footage showed him shooting Rodney in the head, then calling someone to remove the body.

In Max's eyes, there was no way around it. Brighton was going down. Then again, he did have a lot of ties to the community. His power and reach might allow him room to create reasonable doubt in the minds of a jury, if he went through with a trial.

Max shuddered at the thought of what Brighton might do if he decided to check into who sent the video. *Who's to say he's not already doing that?* The realization hit Max like a ton of bricks. That was another thing Sam held over their heads. He had been so busy worrying about the possibility of her outing them to the police that he hadn't thought about the fact that Sam could just as easily feed their names to Brighton and his lawyer.

Would she really do that though? Brighton could have us killed!

Max's heart sank. It was definitely a possibility, especially since he had plotted her murder a few years ago. What would hold her back from seeking vengeance?

A call from his mother halted Max's thought process. He scrunched his face in disgust at the sight of her name flashing on his screen.

He wanted to reject the call but decided he might as well answer. He had nothing else to do. He clicked the Answer button. "What do you want?"

Pauline chuckled. "Is that any way to greet your mother?"

"What is it, Mom?"

Her laughter died down. "Your father and I wanted you to come to dinner."

"Come to dinner? For what?"

Max's parents had made it clear for all his life after his brother Jared was born that they weren't interested in anything he had going on. Why would they want to have dinner with him all of a sudden?

"We'll tell you when we get here. We're starting around seven on Friday."

Chapter 12

Sam moaned as Martell's expert hands traveled up and down her freshly oiled back. His fingers were working wonders in more ways than one. "Mm, yes, right there!" she said, as he reached one of her most tense spots. He took his time kneading out her kinks, then she felt his soft breath on her lower back.

Sam immediately moistened. "Martell, stop playing!" she said, but she wanted nothing more but for him to continue. He gently blew his breath in a back and forth pattern, and it was turning Sam on to no end. She squirmed underneath him, ready for his lips and tongue to explore other areas.

Martell must have decided she had enough, because he eased up off her, then flipped her around so they were facing each other. His penetrating stare burned holes into her soul. She sat up to meet him for a kiss, and he caressed her, holding her soft breasts in his hands.

His kisses trailed lower, his tongue giving extra attention to her sensitive spots, then he went even lower, pulling down her thong as he kissed across her navel. She opened her legs to give him full sight of the feast before him.

He licked his lips, indicating that he was about to dig in.

His head lowered, but before he could take her to ecstasy, a loud knock sounded at her front door. Martell's head popped up, and Sam's vibe was shattered.

"Who is that?" she hissed, covering herself with a pillow. *I swear, he better not have had some woman follow him here!* Her mind went to the fiasco with Dallas. If Martell turned out to be a liar too, there would be hell to pay.

"How am I supposed to know?" Martell asked. "This is your house." He looked upset that their session was interrupted as well. The obnoxious knocking continued. Whoever was on the other side of the door had to be using a blunt object because no way was that someone's fist.

Sam was too pissed to think straight. She snatched a robe from the back of her bedroom door, slid into her slippers, then stalked to the front door, flinging it open to a red-faced McConnell, Brighton's lawyer.

"What the hell are you doing here?" she seethed.

McConnell stammered. "M..ms..Samantha. Brighton wanted me to reach out to you. I called but I wasn't able to get through to your cell phone."

"So you got the bright idea to come to my house?"

McConnell didn't answer.

"What do you want? I already told Brighton I couldn't help him."

McConnell was silent for a moment. "May I come in?"

Sam crossed her arms. "No, you may not. It was rude of you to intrude upon my premises, so I'll return the favor. You can say whatever you have to say from right where you stand, then you can leave."

McConnell cleared his throat. "Very well." He leaned closer, and his soft brown eyes beheld a sincerity that Sam suspected was an act to gain her assistance. "Brighton suspects that Blake Cunningham sent that footage to the police. He wants to know if you will help to prove this."

Sam almost laughed in his face. Blake Cunningham had nothing to do with this, and she knew it. Brighton didn't have a clue that the real person behind his actions being leaked to the press were not one of his political opponents, but Sam's ex boyfriend.

"McConnell, if you suspect Blake, why don't you have someone on your team look into it?"

McConnell cleared his throat again. "We tried, but Blake is difficult to penetrate. We were hoping to try from another angle."

The suggestiveness in his tone cause Sam to cock back her head in disbelief. "You mean to tell me Brighton wants to pimp me out to get dirt on Blake?"

McConnell was stammering again. "Well, no, we just...we wanted you to..."

"You wanted me to seduce him and get him to tell me all his deep dark secrets."

McConnell's ears reddened, but he didn't respond.

"Mm mm mm...Brighton must be in a hell of a predicament."

"Samantha..." She slammed the door in his face.

Sam watched as McConnell trudged back to his vehicle, satisfaction etched across her features, until Martell's voice interrupted her moment.

"You're still dealing with Brighton?"

Sam whirled around, startled at the seriousness of his tone. Martell stood before her, fully clothed, with a hardened expression on his face.

"He's just…He…" It was her turn to get tongue-tied. *No!* Her mind screamed. She was not ready to let go of Martell yet. His bedroom game was on point, and Dallas was gone. If Martell broke things off with her, she would have no one to satisfy her needs.

"Save it, Sam," Martell said, heading toward the door. "He wouldn't feel so comfortable reaching out if you two weren't still connected. I hope it was worth it."

He exited her house and slammed the door behind him.

Though she had no intentions on pursuing a serious relationship with Martell, she still felt bad that her actions had hurt him. One more reason to be pissed at Brighton.

Chapter 13

Shatina had gone to all of her classes so far except Dark Psychology, which was only held once a week. Thursday night, she filed into the classroom along with her other classmates, unsure what to expect from Ted, their instructor.

Class was supposed to start at six, but fifteen minutes passed and Ted hadn't arrived. Unless he had been in the room the whole time. Shatina had no idea what he looked like. If he was there, however, why hadn't he started the class?

"Does anyone know if he canceled?" a student in the back of the small amphitheater asked.

Murmurs could be heard around the room.

Shatina hoped he hadn't canceled because she had been nervous about this class the whole week.

Finally, Ted strode into the room, wheeling a midsized bin with him. He was a tall, African American man with a muscular frame and an imposing demeanor. He wore khakis and dress shoes with a button down shirt, but he was far from a nerd, Shatina could tell. If she wasn't so nervous about how she would do in his class, she would be attracted to him.

Then her face scrunched as she realized he looked familiar. She had seen this man before…where though? Shatina couldn't put her finger on it.

"Good evening," Ted said, a subtle smirk playing on the corners of his lips. "I suppose you're all here for Dark Psychology."

No one responded, but the anticipation could be felt across the room.

"Don't all speak at once," he said with a chuckle, but not the friendly kind. He wasn't scary, but he was definitely intimidating. But also attractive. *Attractively intimidating?* the voice mocked, but Shatina didn't bother to answer.

Ted stroked his goatee in amusement, then shrugged. "Okay, have it your way."

He pointed at a girl sitting in one of the front rows. "You. Hand these out for me." He pulled out two stacks of papers from the bin and handed them to the girl, who looked nervous as she took them in her shaky hands.

Shatina was slightly taken aback by Ted's choice of words. He didn't frame his statement as a question, it was more of a command with expectations that the girl comply. She did.

Shatina learned that the papers the girl was passing out were copies of the syllabus, along with a nondisclosure agreement. "What is this?" she said to herself, wrinkling her nose as she read the agreement.

Ted must have had bionic hearing because he answered her question. "The nondisclosure agreement is clear. Nothing we discuss in this course from this moment on leaves this room. I take the agreements very serious, and if anyone goes against them, you will face harsh consequences."

Shatina didn't like the feeling of this, but she couldn't help but to admit she was intrigued. She stared at the rest of her classmates. There were about fifty of them in total, and many of them looked just as curious as she felt.

Ted waited until all students signed the agreements, then he had them pass them to the end of the row so the girl who handed them out could collect them.

He nodded when she handed him the stack of signed papers, but he didn't thank her.

Ted sifted through each paper, then he looked up and counted how many students were in the room. "Good," he said with a pleased smile. "Next, we have our honor code statement."

He pointed at another girl and told her to come and pass out the honor code statements, which contained a promise to never use the information or methodologies described in the course to manipulate unsuspecting members of society.

Once those were signed, Ted checked them over to make sure no one left theirs blank. "Good," he said when he finished.

"Class dismissed. Read over the syllabus before our next meeting. I expect you all to be ready to hit the ground running."

Everyone stared at each other, but no one dared raise their hand to ask him why he was dismissing a three hour class barely an hour into the session.

Shatina was one of the last students to file out. She looked back at Ted as he locked the door to the amphitheater after the last student exited.

He probably doesn't want to lug that bin around, she reasoned. *But they really gave him the whole amphitheater to himself?*

Ted turned and saw her watching. "Shatina?" he said, and she was taken aback by the fact that he already knew her name. He stepped closer, and everything inside her wanted to step back, or even run away, but she didn't.

"Yes," she forced out, keeping her breathing to a minimum.

"Did you have a question for me?"

He stared into her eyes, looking completely relaxed while she was internally wringing her hands.

"No, I'm fine." She turned to walk away.

"Good," Ted said, as she made it to her car.

Chapter 14

Sam was beyond pissed that not only did Martell break things off with her, but that Brighton had the audacity to think he could come to her with such a request.

"Is that what he thinks of me?"

She wasn't sure why she was so upset with him, seeing that she had no problem sleeping with multiple men simultaneously without a second thought. Still, what right did Brighton think he had over what she did with her body? How dare he make such a suggestion?

A call from her father interrupted Sam's thoughts. "Ugh, not this again."

She decided to answer this time. She couldn't have him showing up unannounced like he did last time. "Hello?"

"Samantha."

She clenched her teeth. "Like I said, it's Sam."

"Right. Sam. Anyway, how have you been?"

Sam blew out a breath. "I've been fine, Dad. How have you been?"

Dexter chose to ignore her impatient tone. "Listen honey, I've been thinking."

Honey? "Thinking about what?"

"I know things are sticky with Brighton's situation, but I may be able to pull a few strings with the judge to help him out."

Sam's eyes narrowed, though she knew Dexter couldn't see her. "And why would I want you to do that?"

Dexter sighed. "Look Sam, I know I haven't been the best father to you over the years…"

Sam snorted.

"But I want us to find a way to rekindle our trust," he continued.

"Rekindle our trust? Do you hear yourself? How do you think I would ever trust you again after all you've done? You haven't shown me anything but the fact that you are the one person on this earth I could never depend on. You destroyed my mother's psyche, not to mention what you did to me."

Dexter fell silent for a moment. "How is your mother doing?"

"How do you think she's doing, Dad! You made her the laughingstock of the whole town. She doesn't even want to show her face anywhere. If there's anyone you should be pestering for a rekindled relationship, it's her. How about you start there?"

"Samantha, that situation is complicated…"

"Didn't I tell you my name was Sam?"

Dexter sighed like he was getting upset.

Go on, do it, Sam dared him with her mind. *Go ahead and say something crazy so I can have an excuse to never talk to you again.*

"Sam…" he started. "Look, this conversation isn't going the way I intended. I'll try back later."

He hung up.

Sam let her phone drop onto her bed. He ended their interaction like a business call. *I'll try back later.* Who did he think he was?

Sam hadn't pulled any schemes against her father, but she wanted to add him to her list. The only thing was, she didn't think that would be such a good idea. Dexter would likely find her out and the whole situation would do more harm than good.

Sam thought back to her childhood. She'd read in her psychology class that the first thing a child learned was to trust their caregivers. She had, until her father destroyed that notion at three years old.

They were home alone in the basement. It was before her father's company took off, so they had to do their own laundry and errands, and there was no nanny to keep Sam company and watch over her during the day.

Sam was helping her father remove the clothes from the washer and put them into the dryer. When they finished and he turned it on, he proposed a game.

"A game?" Three-year-old Sam grew excited at the idea.

Her father knelt to her level. "Do you want to play?" he asked with friendly eyes.

Sam nodded, bouncing up and down in anticipation. He lifted her until she was standing on top of the washing machine, then told her to turn around with her back facing him.

"Okay, here's how we play," he said. "Close your eyes, then when I count to three, I want you to lean back and I'll catch you. Deal?"

Sam thought that was a funny idea for a game, but she went along with it. She closed her eyes, anticipation building for the climactic moment when she fell back into her father's arms.

"Ready?" Her father said. "One…two…three!"

Sam fell back without hesitation and a big smile on her face, but the immediate pain she felt as her head hit the concrete floor caused her to cry out in anguish.

She opened her eyes, feeling dizzy though she was laying down.

Her father stood over her with a cold expression on his face.

"Hey Kiddo. Sorry I had to do that, but you needed to learn."

Sam was too busy crying to ask any questions, so he continued. "You can't trust anyone in this world, understand? I had to learn that the hard way, so I decided to teach you early."

He didn't say anything else after that. He just left her there crying on the floor as he walked up the stairs to watch TV.

When Sam entered the living room, she saw that her kiddie table had a plate with a half sandwich, chocolate chip cookies, and milk sitting on it. She looked at Dexter, who was eating a sandwich of his own. He nodded at her. "Go ahead, I didn't put anything in it."

Sam wasn't sure what that meant, but Dexter said it was okay to eat the food, so she did.

An hour later, her mother came home. She bent to give Sam a hug and kiss but noticed that her nose was bleeding.

"Baby, what happened?" her mother said with concern.

"I fell." Tears filled Sam's eyes.

Dexter was standing at a distance, watching their interaction.

"You fell? How? What happened?"

"I hit my head!" Sam wailed, and her mother immediately began inspecting her. When she found the knot on the back of Sam's head, she turned to Dexter, who held a neutral expression.

"What happened to her?"

He shrugged. "She fell off a slide at the park, but she was running around after, so I thought she was good."

Sam's mother whisked her to the Emergency Room, where they learned she had a concussion. When the nurse asked Sam what happened, she repeated the story Dexter told. She knew it wasn't true though.

When they got home that night, Sam's parents had a huge argument. Her mother, Tracy, screamed at Dexter about how Sam could have died due to his negligence.

At first, Dexter was silent as she yelled, then he blurted out, "What do I care? She's not mine anyway."

Sam's memory was blocked after that moment, but those words replayed in her mind throughout her childhood. She didn't understand them when Dexter first said them, but she later got the picture.

Chapter 15

Max showed up to his parent's house, not sure what to make of their invitation. "Hey," he said, when his mother opened the door.

She gave him a forced smile, which let him know that this dinner had nothing to do with him and everything to do with Jared.

He should have known.

Jared had been the golden child since he was born, though he was currently serving a life sentence in prison. Max's parents still doted on their younger son, as if Max never existed.

Max followed his mother into the kitchen, where dinner was already sitting on the table. There was baked chicken, green beans, and rice. Max never liked his mother's baked chicken because she always seemed to dry it out, but it was one of Jared's favorite meals.

Go figure, he thought.

"Max!" His father shot him a fake smile like the one his mother gave him.

"Hey." Max plopped into his seat, and the family began their meal in awkward silence.

"So, did you get a new car? I noticed the Buick isn't outside anymore," his father said.

Max almost opened his mouth to say he got rid of the Buick over a month ago but decided against it. It wasn't like his father cared whether he had a new car anyway, he was only asking the question to fill space.

"I didn't need two cars anymore. Plus, I needed the cash."

"Needed the cash?" his mother chimed in. "Did you lose your job?"

Max shot her a quizzical glance, before he realized she must still think he worked at the toy store he got fired from at eighteen. Max was twenty one. He had moved out of his parent's house shortly after his first paycheck, and they barely noticed him gone, much less the fact that he only stopped by when he wanted to use the Buick, which was parked in their driveway until he got rid of it.

"No, I didn't," was all he said in response.

They went back to their meal for a few more minutes, until Max's father cleared his throat. "Max, we had something we wanted to ask you."

His mother abruptly stopped her meal and stared at him.

Max fought the urge to roll his eyes. *Here it comes,* he thought. "What is it?"

His father's smile was genuine this time. "We have some good news."

His mother perked up as well.

"About?" Max raised his eyebrow.

"Jared is getting out early," his mother gushed, before his father could spill the beans.

Max's mind was running circles. "Getting out early? I'm pretty sure that's not how it works with a life sentence."

His father's expression slightly faltered. "Well, his appeal was granted, and his conviction was changed to involuntary rather than voluntary. They're letting him out due to overpopulation and good behavior."

Max didn't bother to address that. "What does this have to do with me?"

They both looked nervous now. His mother glanced at his father, and he gave a nod for her to take over.

"Well Max...Of course you know we would be happy to have Jared released to our home, but he requested to stay with you."

Chapter 16

After the incident when she was three years old, Dexter mostly acted normally around Sam. He never told her directly he knew he wasn't her father, and if Sam hadn't heard her parent's argument she never would have known.

Once her teen years hit, however, he began acting differently toward her mother Tracy. He would stay out for long hours at night and they would always get into arguments. Tracy would accuse him of all sorts of things, and Dexter would deny it. Then he would go back to a nice, carefree demeanor until he started staying out late again. It wasn't until Sam's eighteenth birthday that things blew up in Dexter's face.

It was revealed that night that Dexter had slept with not one, but all of Tracy's friends. Martine, Tracy's closest friend, blurted out that she was pregnant with Dexter's child, and all hell broke loose. She demanded that Dexter leave Tracy like he promised her he would, and that was when their other friends jumped in the argument. Apparently, Dexter had given each of them a similar promise, but only Martine had a leg to stand on since she was pregnant. They all wanted him because his company was making a ton of money at the time, and none of them were as well off as Dexter and Tracy.

Needless to say, Sam's birthday was ruined. While Tracy and Dexter were going through their divorce and Dexter was enduring a lawsuit from Martine, Sam grew closer to one of her friends, Lacey. She and Lacey would talk for hours about all of Sam's feelings about the situations.

Martine ended up losing the baby, so Dexter didn't have to pay child support, but Tracy went through with the divorce. Since then, she fell into a rut of depression, barely getting out of bed for most days in the beginning. Nowadays she was taking better care of herself, but the pain of the situation was still evident.

Sam's fist balled as she thought of how Lacey betrayed her in the worst way. First, she made a move on Max, which led to their subsequent breakup. If Sam hadn't caught them in the middle of their make out session, Max and Lacey would have slept together. Max apologized profusely, and Sam took him back, but then the feelings of resentment grew too strong, so she started sleeping with Brighton, then left Max altogether for him.

She and Lacey never rekindled their friendship, and Sam had almost forgotten about the girl, until she caught her out with Dexter one night, coming out of the same hotel Sam was entering with Martell.

Dexter and Lacey didn't see Sam that night, but she had all the information she needed to take Lacey down. She had her contact track both of their cell phones and email addresses, and that was how she found out Dexter had given Lacey the necklace.

It held sentimental value, which would make Sam's revenge that much sweeter.

The necklace cost thousands of dollars, but what was inside the locket that hung from it meant more to Lacey. It was a picture of her and her father, who she had lost in a house fire when she was seven. Sam knew how much the locket meant to Lacey, because the picture was the only thing she had left of her father.

Too bad that memory was about to be extinguished.

Chapter 17

Shatina sat with her classmates in the amphitheater for the Dark Psychology class. She had read over the syllabus, which was only a page long, the same night Ted handed them out. Essentially, all course materials were held in the bin Ted brought with him on the first day, and all articles they would be reading would return to the bin after each class session. They were allowed to take notes on the articles, but not to remove them from the classroom. Shatina looked up one of them on the school's database and found that the articles Ted chose for their class weren't in the school's system. The only way to access them was to pay a fee, and she wasn't doing that. She would stick with the free copies Ted gave them during class.

It was five past six, and Ted hadn't arrived. Shatina knew he was on campus though, because the doors to the amphitheater were open for everyone to file in.

The anticipation could be felt in the room as conversations were being held about when Ted would show up, and what he would have them do today for their first official lecture. Shatina guessed that Ted wasn't the PowerPoint type.

Five minutes later, Ted strode into the room carrying a stack of note cards and shut the doors behind him. "Good evening," he said. "Tonight will be our first official session. I trust that each of you have read the syllabus and understand the terms. Any questions?"

He looked around the room and no one raised their hand. "Good. You," he pointed to a student in the second row of seats. "Pass out these notecards."

He pointed at another woman in the first row. "While she's passing those out, you pass out these articles."

Shatina fought the urge to suck her teeth. She didn't like the way he pointed people out and commanded them to do things for him, not to mention that he only seemed to choose women to comply with his demands.

The women wordlessly took the notecards and articles and passed them to each row. The notecards were blank. Once the last person received their materials, Ted spoke.

"As you hold these cards in your hands, I want each of you to take a moment to think back. Answer this question: what's the worst thing you've ever done, and gotten away with it? While you're thinking take a look at the article you received."

Shatina stared at the article. It was titled, *Is Everyone Capable of Murder?* A sense of apprehension filled her body. She wasn't sure she wanted to stay for this lecture, especially with the various situations looming over her head.

Ted gave them forty five minutes to read the article and write their answers on the notecards.

One student was brave enough to raise his hand and ask whether they had to put their names on the notecards, and that question caused Ted to smile.

"Of course not," he said. "Everything in this course is confidential, after all."

Once that statement was made, people seemed to relax. Shatina contemplated what to write on her card. She had done a lot of bad things, but had she really gotten away with them? Sure, she never got caught, but was not getting caught and getting away the same thing? Shatina thought not. The weight of her prior actions stuck with her every day, and oftentimes she couldn't help but wonder if the reason her life was so crazy at this moment was because of all the dirt she had done.

Still, she knew she had to write something on her card. She scrawled out her answer, barely making it legible, turned it over so the other blank side was facing up, and passed it down the row when Ted called time.

Once the notecards were in his hands, Ted shuffled them, then took a deep breath and cracked his neck. "Hm. Let's see what truths you brave souls unleashed today."

He pulled a card from the stack, squinting to read it, then sucked his teeth. "Really? I lost my neighbor's cat? Come on guys, I was expecting something juicy."

He shuffled again, then pulled another card. "I stole fifty dollars from my grandmother's purse. Ooh, badass." Ted looked impressed at that one.

He shuffled again and pulled out a third card. "What does this say?" He scrunched his face to read it, and Shatina's heart dropped. She knew he had her card in front of him. Ted whistled, then read the card out loud. "Whoowee, we have a winner! I poisoned my sister." He tossed the rest of the stack onto the long wooden table on the small stage he was standing on, still holding Shatina's confession in his hands. "Hm, let's play a game. If I can guess whose card this is, would you have the guts to tell us?"

Shatina's eyes widened, and her breathing became labored. She hadn't expected Ted to pick out her card, much less try to figure out who had written it. This wasn't fair.

No sooner than she had the thought, Ted spoke again. "Let me guess...Shatina."

Her entire body was a bundle of nerves, but she fought to maintain an even composure. A few heads whipped toward her, but other students didn't know who she was.

Ted was staring at Shatina as if he could see through her. "It was you, wasn't it?"

"Why would you think that?" Shatina asked, with the straightest face she could muster.

Ted shrugged, a hint of a smirk playing at his lips. "Just a hunch." He turned his attention to the room at large. "Okay, let's do it like this: raise your hand if you have a sister."

Over half the room's hands were raised.

"Put your hand down if your sister is younger."

Multiple hands went down.

"Put it down if she's older."

People looked confused at that one, but everyone except Shatina and another male student were left standing.

Ted's smirk grew more pronounced. "Well, well, well...here we are. Two students left, and one of them was my lucky guess. What do you guys think?"

He paced the floor, and Shatina and the male student shared an awkward glance.

A separate student raised her hand.

Ted nodded.

"Why did you have us put our hands down based on whether our sister was younger or older?"

Ted paused his pacing, then shrugged. "Statistics," he offered, then began pacing again.

Shatina knew that answer wasn't correct. He somehow knew what she had done. She didn't know how he knew it, but he knew it. Shatina had noticed on the first day of class that Ted looked familiar, but she couldn't put her finger on where she had seen him before. Once she figured that out, she would know how he knew.

Ted focused on the male student whose hand was still raised. "Charles, answer this question: does your twin sister go to this school?"

Charles nodded.

Ted clapped his hands. "Bingo! I was right, then. Shatina did it."

"Wha...that doesn't mean anything!" Shatina stammered, before she could stop herself.

Ted, and her classmates, focused on her. "Doesn't it, though?" Ted said, his smile now sinister.

"Your calculations were totally arbitrary," she said, standing up for herself.

"Yet I came to the right conclusion," Ted countered.

Shatina didn't respond.

"Go ahead, admit it."

"I'm not admitting anything."

"It's not like you killed her."

She almost opened her mouth to ask how he knew that, but Ted continued.

"If you would have killed her, you wouldn't have written that down on your notecard." The class broke out in whispers, and Ted gestured with his hands as if to calm them down. "Chill guys, Shatina's twin sister is alive and well, though I would argue that she probably goes to a school that is at least a hundred miles away."

A few students laughed in response to Ted's remark, but Shatina felt anger and shame coursing through her veins.

"What is the point of this activity?" she asked.

Ted was undeterred by the sharpness of her tone. "To prove the conclusion of the article correct. I knew at least half of you would object to the idea that anyone is capable of murder, so I figured a real life example would help you see the light…" He focused on the rest of the class. "Or in Shatina's case, the darkness."

Shatina didn't know how to feel. She could only imagine what her classmates thought of her, though she never admitted that she had poisoned her sister. *You didn't deny it either though,* the voice said.

Shatina didn't like Ted. Unfortunately, she still had the rest of the semester to deal with him. The rest of the lecture went without incident. Ted started a debate about the contents of the article, and a lot of her classmates got really into it, but Shatina barely heard anything that was said. All she could think about was what Ted had done to her.

Why? Why would he single her out? And how did he know what she did?

***

While Shatina was driving back home from class, Shatara called her phone.

She was so startled by the irony of the situation that she answered. "Hello?"

"Hey sis, what are you up to?"

Shatina turned down a side street. "Heading home from class."

"How was it? I just got out of class too. I'm walking to my dorm." The sounds of movement surrounding Shatara let Shatina know that her sister was indeed walking somewhere.

"How was your class?" Shatina asked.

Shatara sighed. "It was annoying. It's a three hour class, and my teacher bored us to tears."

Shatina snorted. "Ours certainly didn't."

"Oh really? What happened?"

Shatina paused. She wasn't sure if she should tell Shatara what happened because she didn't want to reopen old wounds, but since she had been longing for a connection with her sister for a while, she decided to have at it. "He had us write on a notecard the worst thing we had ever done."

"Huh? Why would he do that?" Shatara sounded confused.

"It's a Dark Psychology class."

"Why are you taking a class like that?"

"Seth signed us up, and I didn't want to drop it." Shatina turned down another street. She was almost home.

"Oh. Okay, gotcha. What did you write on your card?"

Shatina remained silent. She wasn't sure she should tell Shatara now. A moment ago, it was a good idea, but now, not so much.

Shatara answered for her. "You must have told him what you did to me."

Shatina remained silent again.

"Did he make you read it aloud?"

"Worse," Shatina blurted out. "He guessed it was me."

"What?" Shatara sounded like she was taken aback. "How did he guess?"

Shatina rolled her eyes as she pulled up to her apartment. "He said he guessed by using statistics, but I know that's not true. I don't know how he figured it out, but it's bothering me."

"Understandable. I would be bothered too, but sis, don't let him get in your head. What happened is in the past. We all have flaws, myself included."

Shatina was blown away by Shatara's response. She killed her engine and sat there, the weight of the situation now gone from her chest.

Maybe talking to Shatara was a good idea after all.

They chatted more about their days for another half hour, then called it a night. Shatina felt a new sense of comfort in opening up to her sister.

Chapter 18

Sam was in the middle of an online chat with a new romantic prospect when a call from Brighton interrupted her flow. She was still pissed he ruined her fling with Martell by sending McConnell to her door, so she answered. Brighton was about to get a piece of her mind.

"Hello?"

"Sam…what's going on with you?" He had the audacity to sound upset.

"What's going on with me? The better question is, what's going on with you that you feel the need to send your lawyer to my door to help with your case. You need to hire another one at this point because McConnell is clearly wasting your money."

"Sam, cut the crap. You know why I sent him. You're smart. You know how to figure things out."

Sam knew exactly what he meant by *figure things out*. He couldn't have McConnell do anything illegal, or the evidence would be inadmissible. Sam had ways of finding information, however.

"Goodbye, Brighton." She wasn't going to hang up, but she wanted to hear him beg.

"Sam, wait. Please!"

She smiled, then forced a frown so her voice wouldn't betray her emotion. "Why should I help you, Brighton? It's not like you care about me."

"What do you mean? Sam, we've been together for almost two years. I love you."

The seriousness of his tone threw her off, but Brighton's words shocked Sam even further. She never had a man tell her he loved her, and Brighton sounded like he meant it. She wasn't sure how to handle that, so she filed it in the back of her mind but focused on the more pressing matter.

"You love me, huh? Then why did you cheat?"

Brighton pretended to be clueless. "What? Cheat? I don't know what you're…"

Sam cut him off. "Letricia Samuels. Fifteen hundred Cedarwood Terrace, Apartment three B."

"Sam…"

"I saw footage of you two together, Brighton. Don't try to deny it."

He was silent for a long moment, then sighed. "Sam, I'm sorry. I know you won't believe me but what I did with her meant nothing. She's not…"

The automated voice cut off Brighton's words, telling them they had less than a minute left in the call.

Brighton continued. "Sam, I really am sorry," he repeated. "When I get out of here, I will make it up to you, that's a promise. I just need…"

Sam cut him off again. "I don't feel like having this conversation right now. We'll chat later." She hung up before he could get another call in.

A few minutes later, a call from McConnell came in, but Sam ignored it, figuring it was Brighton trying to do a three-way.

Chapter 19

Max's parents were pissed at him, to say the least. Dinner did not end well. When his mother asked if Jared could be released to Max's apartment, Max said no.

"What do you mean, no?" his mother said.

It wasn't that Max had anything against Jared, it was that he had way bigger fish to fry at this moment in his life. He wasn't adding Jared to the list of his problems.

"How could you say no to your own brother?" Max's father asked.

"Why doesn't he want to stay with you two?" Max shot back.

"We don't know," his mother said. "But he specifically requested you, Max. You can't just turn your back on him."

"I'm not turning my back on him, but he's not my responsibility either. He's your son, not mine."

Both of Max's parents looked taken aback at that remark.

"Max," his father tried again. "Can't you just let him stay for a few months?"

"When is he getting out?" Max asked. Maybe there was a way he could swing it, if the date was after Thanksgiving.

His mother's expression softened. "Within the next few weeks. Thank you, Max. We know we could never repay you, but..."

"I can't take him in," Max said, before she could finish her speech.

"Then why did you ask when he was getting out?" His father asked in an accusatory tone.

Max had had enough. "Look, neither of you care what's going on with my life, so don't pretend to now, but I've got too much going on to be worrying about Jared." He stood from the table because he was sure he was no longer welcome.

"Max, where is he going to stay!" His mother looked as if she was close to tears. "He has nowhere else to go."

"He should have thought about that before he committed murder."

"It wasn't murder, it was..."

"It was murder, Dad. Stop the BS." Max was tired of his parents. With the way they carried on when it came to Jared, it was no wonder he was serving a life sentence. Granted, the judge had offered the possibility of parole after ten years, but still. Jared murdered that guy in cold blood. Max's parents took out a second mortgage and got Jared a good enough lawyer to raise doubts in the minds of the jury. He ended up with a voluntary manslaughter conviction, which Max's parents fought to have appealed and turned into involuntary manslaughter. Which was why Jared was eligible for release.

Max didn't bother to question whether they would have done such a thing for him.

***

A month had passed since his conversation with his parents, and Max wasn't sure if Jared had changed his mind about staying with them or what, because he hadn't heard from them. Max was on his way from delivering the last of his pills to a client when he got a text from Sam, calling another meeting.

I feel like we need a check in, she had written, with a silly face emoji.

Max wasn't in the mood for games, but he texted back to answer when and where. He was pissed all over again when she told him she wanted to meet at the cabin in less than an hour.

"Here we go with this drama," he said, and headed to the cabin.

Chapter 20

Sam threw a curve ball and arrived at the meeting early this time. She wanted to see who showed up first, Max or Shatina.

She held a satisfied smile on her face until she saw Shatina's car pull up. Sam had her heart set on Max getting to the cabin first.

Shatina remained in her vehicle until Max showed up, ten minutes later.

Max looked pissed as he got out of his car and slammed the door. Shatina exited her vehicle as well and stared at him.

"What's wrong with you?" she asked.

Max shook his head, his jaw squared. "I'll tell you about it later."

Shatina nodded.

Sam was heated. What did he mean, he would tell her about it later? The last she had seen, Shatina and Max were at odds. When did they make up? Sam didn't like this at all. She stood from her seat as Max and Shatina entered the cabin through the front door, which Sam had propped open in preparation for their arrival.

Neither of them addressed her as they sat at the table.

"What's this about?" Shatina asked in a rude tone. "I have a test to study for."

"Yeah, and I have to get back to work myself," Max agreed. "Some of us have better things to do with our lives than to be here playing games."

Max's words and tone of voice hurt her, but Sam didn't dare show it.

"Need I remind you two that I have evidence that could make both of your lives much more complicated than they already are?"

"Trust me, we don't need a reminder," Shatina said.

"Just get to the point, Sam," Max said. "Why did you call us here?"

Sam smirked, though she was still put off by his tone. Something outside of her calling this meeting was bothering Max. She wanted to know what it was.

She let out a deep breath. "Like I said, I felt like we needed to check in. It's the first week of October, and Thanksgiving is coming soon. Do each of you understand your duties at the gala?"

Sam had provided them with a map of Lacey's parent's mansion. Her mother remarried after her father died, and her stepfather was a millionaire. Lacey still lived with them.

"Yes, we have the layout of the place memorized. Was that all?"

Sam decided that Max was doing entirely too much tonight with his attitude.

"Yes, that's all for Miss Shatina. I'll have both of your server uniforms next month, but Max, I need to speak with you for a second."

Shatina shot Sam a strange look, but she didn't bother to stick around once she was dismissed. She nodded at Max, then headed to her car to drive off.

Max stayed at the table, a sullen expression on his face.

"What's got you so upset?" Sam asked in a sweet tone.

Max snorted. "What do you care?"

"Max, we do have history."

"Indeed we do, which is why I'm here in the first place."

Sam opened her mouth then closed it. "Okay, I won't press you, but I want you to know that whatever is bothering you, I'm here to talk about it."

Max scoffed. "Yeah, I bet you are." The sarcasm in his tone was not missed.

Chapter 21

Shatina went straight home after the meeting with Sam and Max, then proceeded to make herself a light dinner. She prepared a Caesar salad along with some spicy chili. She had just turned off the pot for the chili when she heard a knock on her front door.

"Who is that?" she asked. She stared through the peephole, and it was Max. He must have meant what he said when he told her they would talk later.

She opened the door. "Hey," she said.

"Hey." Max looked like he was unsure of himself. "Do you mind if I come in?"

"Sure." Shatina gestured for Max to enter her apartment, then closed the door behind him.

"It smells good in here," he remarked.

"I just finished cooking."

He stopped in his tracks. "Oh, I didn't mean to interrupt your dinner. I'm sorry."

Shatina gestured to let him know it was fine. "You're good. Are you hungry?"

Max looked surprised at her offer, but he nodded. "Sure. Thanks!"

Shatina offered him a half smile, then they entered her kitchen. She fixed herself and Max bowls of salad and chili, then brought out the utensils and napkins.

"Did you want some sweet tea?" she asked. "All I have outside of that is water."

Max smiled. "Sweet tea is fine."

Shatina nodded and poured them both a glass.

They ate in silence for a few moments before Shatina broke the silence. "What's bothering you? You seemed pissed at the meeting."

Max's shoulders tensed, but he calmed himself. "Just got a lot going on." His eyes went back and forth.

"Such as?" Shatina asked with a raised eyebrow.

Max took a bite of his salad, then sighed. "My brother's getting released from prison and my parents asked if he could stay with me. I said no."

Shatina's mind was swimming. "Brother? I didn't know you had a brother. What was he in prison for? And why did you say no? Because of what we have going on with Sam?"

Max nodded. "I didn't want him involved in this mess. He went in for *involuntary manslaughter*." Max used his fingers for air quotes for those last two words, which let Shatina know he didn't agree with his brother's verdict.

"At least he's getting a second chance," she offered.

Max scoffed. "Something tells me that Jared won't see it that way. I think he's a sociopath. Or a psychopath, one."

Shatina blinked. "Why would you think that?"

Max shrugged. "A few things he did while we were growing up, plus the reason he was sentenced to prison."

"What kinds of things?" Shatina was hoping he wouldn't start rattling off a list similar to things she had done for revenge on her enemies.

"Killing animals, accidentally setting fire to our parent's first house, you know, the usual."

Shatina relaxed slightly. She and Jared weren't the same.

Max continued. "The worst part was that our parents never suspected him for any of it. They immediately blamed it all on me."

Shatina was intrigued. "Why is that?"

Max shrugged again. "It's complicated."

Chapter 22

After his conversation with Shatina, Max grew curious as to whether Jared had gotten out yet. It had been a while since the argument, so if his mother's words were correct, Jared should have been released.

Had he changed his mind about staying with them?

Max drove toward their house. He planned to knock on the door and ask if Jared was home, then leave when he got his answer.

When he got to the neighborhood, he saw that Jared was home indeed. Jared was standing on the front porch, smoking a cigarette and talking to Max's uncle Marcus, the one who had gotten him out of trouble with the police for his attempted murder and kidnapping of Sam a few years ago. A few other cars were parked out front, which let Max know his parents had thrown a party.

A party he wasn't invited to.

Max felt something indescribable on the inside. He wanted to break something, or hurt someone, but he didn't know what to do.

He didn't want to do anything too stupid that would get him locked up, but he needed to find a release.

He texted Anthony, a guy who distributed pills a few blocks over.

Hey, you still got that?

Anthony wrote back less than a minute later. *Thought you were good?*

Max was good, originally. He had meant what he said to his client Gerard when he told him he was done selling once he ran out, but he was contacting Anthony for a different reason. *I just need something for the night.*

You sure?

Yup.

Anthony sent him a location and Max arrived there shortly. He handed Anthony the money and Anthony gave him four pills.

"Take care of yourself, brainiac," Anthony said, and that only made Max feel worse. His drug dealing associates saw more in him than his parents ever had. They often called him names like *brainiac* or *egg head* to indicate that they admired his intelligence and to let him know he wasn't about the street life. They were right and Max knew it, but it wasn't like he had other influences to push him to something better.

Max took all four pills when he got home. He didn't even know what kind they were. He just hoped whatever Anthony gave him wouldn't kill him.

He felt a little woozy an hour later, then an earsplitting headache arose until he released his insides in his toilet.

After that, he fell asleep.

When he awoke the next morning, he felt the same as he had before he took the pills. "Just my luck, even drugs don't help." He rolled back over and dozed off again.

Chapter 23

Shatina was sick of Ted. October was coming to a close, which meant they only had about a month and a half left in the semester. She was passing all of her classes with A's, except Dark Psychology. Ted's graded assignments consisted of three papers throughout the semester, the first two being worth twenty percent of their grade each, and the last one taking the other sixty percent. The first paper was on the article about everyone being capable of murder. Shatina thought she had done a good job, until it was returned with an *F* circled at the top and over a hundred comments in the margins, scrutinizing every line she had written.

"Is this the only class he teaches?" She said, when she thought about how much time he had to have taken to have given such thorough feedback on a three page paper.

The second paper was six pages, and it involved them watching a video of a person being questioned by police for a crime they allegedly didn't do. They were told to study the body language of the suspect based on insights given by another article Ted assigned and decide whether they were telling the truth.

Ted said they would be given bonus points if they were correct in their assessment, but the actual grade for the paper would be based on their reasoning. It was a cool assignment, and if Shatina didn't hate her professor so much, she would have enjoyed completing it. Instead, she found herself scrutinizing every word of her second paper as Ted had done with her first one, trying to make it perfect. She worked on the paper for a whole week, when she was normally able to bang out an assignment like this in a matter of hours.

Unfortunately, her efforts were in vain. Ted awarded her ten bonus points for being correct in her assessments - the suspect was guilty - but she still got an *F*. The paper was swarming with comments, just like the first one, and Ted's final comment pissed her off.

Nice try, but your reasoning is all over the place.

If her reasoning was all over the place, how did she come to the right conclusion? Shatina decided she had enough. The other students might be intimidated by Ted and his imposing demeanor, but she wasn't. She had been on the first day of class, but that feeling was long gone. Ted was going to get a piece of her mind tonight.

She heard a few other students speaking in hushed tones about their excitement of the course. Both of them had gotten A's on their papers. Shatina knew one of them, Tarah. Seth had tutored Tarah last semester when she was taking another psych class. Shatina had seen a copy of a paper Tarah had him look over for her, and she was a horrible writer. No way had she improved that much over the summer. This had to be personal, but Shatina had no idea why.

She stood outside the door of the amphitheater while the other students filed out, some of them saying goodbye to her as they exited. It was chilly due winter swiftly approaching, but Shatina didn't care. She stood there shivering as she waited for Ted to lock up.

He finally emerged, pulling a scully over his head before locking the door.

Shatina cut to the chase. "Ted?" She took a step closer.

Ted finished locking the door, then turned to face her. "Yes, Shatina?"

"Why did you give me an *F* on my paper?"

He stared her down. "Exactly why I said. Your reasoning skills were all over the place."

"But I got the answer right," she shot back. "How was my reasoning so bad if I came to the right conclusion? Especially considering your lack of reasoning on the second day of class when it came to what happened with my sister."

Shatina realized after her last statement that she just outed herself, but she didn't care. The gloves were off, and Ted was about to get this work, verbally at least.

Instead of taking her tone and body language seriously, Ted smiled in amusement.

This infuriated Shatina even more.

"Shatina," he began, taking a step closer to her and lowering his tone. "You would undoubtedly get off if you were ever questioned by police for murder, but in my class, your grade still stands. Take it as it is and do better next time."

With those words, he backed up and strode off, whistling as he walked.

Shatina wanted to slap that cocky look off his face. Where did she know him from? If she could figure that out, she could get him.

Get him? the voice said. *Haven't you gotten enough people?*

That halted Shatina's thought process, but it didn't change the fact that she wished she had unenrolled from this course.

99

Chapter 24

The gala was only a week away, so it was time for one final meeting. Sam had Max and Shatina's uniforms pressed, then she wrapped them both in plastic so they wouldn't get damaged or stained. The garments were held up by hangers in the rear passenger seat of Sam's jeep.

She arrived at the cabin twenty minutes late, much to Max and Shatina's chagrin.

"Which one is mine?" Shatina asked as soon as Sam walked in the door holding the uniforms. "I have somewhere to be."

Max looked equally antsy.

Sam chuckled. "Hold your horses, will you? We need to go over the final details."

"You already gave us the details," Max said. "We go in, pretend to be servers on the main floor, then find a way to get upstairs to Lacey's bedroom. Once we steal the necklace, we leave."

Sam pursed her lips as he spoke. "Good boy," she said with a smile when he finished.

"I want you to bring the necklace back to this cabin when you leave the mansion."

"What, do you own this place or something?" Shatina asked, and the look in her eyes told Sam she had been wondering about the cabin for a while. Sam decided to toy with her. "You mean Max never told you? We used to sneak here all the time to get our freak on."

Shatina made a face, but Max didn't flinch.

"Whatever, Sam. Can we go now?"

Sam was thoroughly enjoying the power she had over both of them, so she decided to turn it up a notch, just for fun.

"Yes, you may leave, but I feel the need to remind you of one thing: if you leave that mansion without the necklace, I will forward the rest of the footage to the police."

That statement took the wind out of both of their sails, Sam could tell.

Shatina spoke next. "How do we know you won't release it anyway?"

Sam pursed her lips. "You'll just have to trust me."

Max wasn't ready to back down either. "We need more than that. Give us something, Sam."

Sam saw the exasperation in his eyes, and it made her feel bad. She decided to alleviate his fears. "My contact has the only copy of the footage, and I've instructed him to delete it once the job is done."

"Who's your contact?" they asked in unison.

Sam grinned. "Come on now, you know I can't tell you that." She turned to Max. "By the way, you really need to get better security for your cloud. I learned way more about you than I wanted to by hacking into your system." She turned to Shatina. "You too. Such pretty handwriting, girl."

Shatina's jaw dropped. "You read my notebook?"

"I thought you had somewhere to be?" Sam said with another smirk. "Besides, it's Max's fault. He's the one who uploaded photocopies to his cloud when he stole it from you."

Shatina turned to Max in anger, and that was when Sam decided her work was done for the night.

She watched them argue back and forth as she walked to her jeep, then sped off.

Chapter 25

Shatina and Max entered the gala on Thanksgiving night. Shatina made up a bogus excuse for her parents as to why she would be late for dinner, but thankfully, they bought it. She looked at Max before they lined up with the other servers. Her eyes scanned the huge ballroom filled with beautifully decorated tables and chairs, before she asked him if he was ready.

"Yup," he said with a nod.

They took their places in the straight line of servers, false identification cards in both of their pockets.

Sam had explained that they had to present themselves to Lacey's head butler before they were searched for weapons and their ID's were checked. Once they were vetted, they would go through a brief training, then the guests would begin to arrive.

Shatina took in the gold and white decor. Each table had a white tablecloth, with gold utensils, plates, and napkins. The wine glasses also had a gold rim. The huge ceiling was adorned with golden chandeliers, and the walls contained paintings which had to be thousands of dollars each.

Shatina reasoned that the ballroom alone was bigger than her parents' entire house.

The head butler, Augustus, arrived, and Shatina almost snickered when she saw him, because his face matched his name. He was an older man with white hair that was neatly pressed. His face was expressionless.

"Good evening," he said in a strong, but even tone. "I trust that each of you has been acquainted with your duties for the evening. You will ensure that no guest has to ask for their glass or plate to be refilled. Anywhere assistance is needed, you are to provide it. Any request that is made, you are to fulfill it. Understand?"

Soft murmurs of agreement could be heard around the room.

"Very well. I will be overseeing the night's events, but don't hesitate to ask a question if you have one."

The look on his face clearly forbade any such question.

Shatina rolled her eyes.

Within a half hour, the place was already filling up. It was a pretty easy job since most people seemed like they just wanted to have a good time. The DJ was playing soft music as the dinner unfolded, but Shatina and Max planned to make their move when it was time for everyone to hit the dance floor. There were over thirty servers and almost two hundred guests, so Shatina hoped it would be easy for them to slip up to Lacey's room and get the necklace. Sam guessed that the bedroom would be unlocked and the necklace would be in the jewelry box she kept in her walk in closet. Shatina hoped she was right.

Shatina and Max did their jobs, filling and refilling glasses and plates, and being on their best behavior. They each received compliments from various guests, though some of them became more belligerent with the increase of alcohol in their systems.

Finally, the music changed to hip hop and dance type tunes. Shatina and Max's time was near.

<h1 style="text-align:center">Chapter 26</h1>

Max had spotted the staircase leading to the wing that contained Lacey's bedroom when he made himself available to one of the chefs. He was asked to carry one of the large turkeys that had been prepared for the evening, so he was able to see that the staircase was easily accessible. He'd also kept his eyes on Augustus throughout the night. At first, Augustus was everywhere, but as the night wore on and no incidents broke out, the man seemed to relax. He started having a few drinks himself and chatting with Lacey's mom and stepfather, who Max had searched for online to see what they looked like.

Max also noted the security detail who were posted around the party. He counted six men, but most of them seemed pretty relaxed. If he and Shatina could slip away without being noticed, they could make their move.

The time finally came. Shatina shot Max a nod, and he gave her one back to indicate he was ready. She pointed her finger toward the kitchen door, indicating she was about to head for the staircase.

Max gave her a thumbs up, then gestured to let her know he would follow.

Shatina refilled one of the guests drinks, and it just so happened that her bottle was now empty. Perfect opportunity to go to the kitchen then slip upstairs without anyone noticing.

She moved so discreetly, Max would have sworn she was supposed to be going back there. Unfortunately, one of the security officers happened to be walking near the kitchen, so he approached her.

Max could tell from Shatina's body language that she was nervous so he approached them as well. "Was that Cabernet?" he shouted over the music at Shatina, gesturing at her bottle.

The officer looked at the empty bottle as well, then nodded. After that, he was on his way.

"What did he say to you?" Max asked Shatina.

She looked grateful for his interception.

"He asked where I was going and I froze up. I second guessed myself." Her eyes filled with tears and Max knew it was more due to nerves than actual fear.

"You're good." He placed his hand on her shoulder. "You know what? I'll go first, and you meet me. If I don't see you within two minutes I'll head to Lacey's bedroom myself."

Shatina stared at him for a moment before she agreed. "Okay."

Max took her empty bottle so he would have an excuse to be in the area, and handed her his, which was half full. Shatina hung around, refilling glasses while Max slipped away. He ditched the bottle in a trash bin near the kitchen door, then looked around. There were a few other servers chatting in the kitchen as they grabbed more bottles of various wines. No one was paying attention to him.

Max figured the coast was clear, so he headed for the stairwell. He was in the middle of the foyer when Augustus' voice filled the area. "Where are you going?" he asked. Max stopped short, getting tongue-tied just as Shatina had with the security officer.

Chapter 27

Shatina inched out of the ballroom just in time to hear Augustus ask where Max was going. Thankfully, this would be an easy workaround.

"There you are!" she called out to Augustus. "Augustus, sir, the host is asking to speak with you."

Augustus looked flustered, but he immediately went back into the ballroom.

Max and Shatina stared at each other.

"Nice save," Max said, visibly relaxing.

"No biggie," Shatina said with a smile. "You literally just did the same thing for me."

Max cocked his head toward the stairwell. "Shall we?"

Shatina nodded. "It's now or never but let me get rid of this bottle first."

They walked into the kitchen just as two other servers were coming out.

"Hey!" said Malcolm, one of the other guys. "This party is crazy right?"

Shatina and Max smiled and nodded, playing off their nervousness.

Malcolm continued. "These folks are laced with dough. Fifteen hundred is a nice wad of cash, but I think they could have given us at least two grand, am I right?" He smiled.

"Right," Shatina and Max agreed in unison.

"Hey," the other guy, Tyler said as he leaned closer. "Some of these bottle of wine are worth over a hundred and fifty dollars. They have so many, they won't notice a few missing." He winked to let them know he had stolen some bottles.

"Whoa, man, that's bold," Max commented, but Shatina could tell he was trying to find a way to end the conversation so they could get moving.

"Right," Shatina cut in. "Thankfully we can leave soon. I'm so ready to blow this place."

Max cut a glance at her, probably because of her change in accent and tone of voice, but he didn't say anything.

"Right, well you guys enjoy your evening," said Malcolm. "Hey Nicolas, maybe we should hang out sometime."

Max froze up for a second, then seemed to remember that he was supposed to be Nicolas. He blinked and snapped out of it. "Yeah, right man. Totally. Let's exchange numbers at the end."

The servers all parked their cars in the same area, so it would be easy to catch up with Malcolm and Tyler, which Shatina already knew Max had no intentions on doing.

"Cool," Tyler said. "Well, we better get back in there before that Augustus dude comes looking. He's already been back here at least four times, the uptight prick."

Shatina rolled her eyes. "Tell me about it. I went to the bathroom and he practically frisked me."

Tyler raised his brow. "Wow, well if he touched you, that's totally a lawsuit. I'd pursue it. You might get a nice chunk of change for that."

Shatina's eyes widened. "Wow, I never even thought of that. Totally sexual harassment, right?"

Tyler and Malcolm nodded. "I'd kill to be a chick right now," Malcolm said. Then he turned to Max. "Okay man, see you in a few."

"See you."

Tyler and Malcolm went back into the ballroom and Shatina broke out into a fit of giggles.

Max chuckled too. "Girl, you are something else."

"What?" Shatina shrugged. "We're playing a part, right? Why not add a few embellishments?"

"A British accent though?" Max said, which caused her to laugh again.

When they calmed down, Max gestured toward the stairwell and Shatina followed suit. They made it to the top of the stairs without incident.

Now it was time to navigate through the darkened hallways to Lacey's room.

Chapter 28

As Shatina and Max crept down the dark hallway, being careful not to make too much noise, Max stopped short. "Wait," he whispered. "Did you see Lacey tonight? She's not wearing the necklace is she?"

Shatina shook her head. "No, that was the first thing I looked out for."

Max relaxed. "Great."

They moved in silence and got halfway to her room, before they heard whistling in the hallway, and saw a flashlight in the distance.

"Shoot!" Max hissed. They should have known there would be at least one security officer upstairs too.

"What should we do?" Shatina asked.

Max thought fast. There was a room off to the left. He prayed it was open. He gestured to Shatina and dashed toward the door, twisting the knob. Thankfully it opened right up into a full bathroom. Max quickly and quietly shut the door behind them. From the sounds of the whistles, the security officer was about to pass them. He stopped short in front of their door and the whistling stopped. "Oh here's the bathroom. Finally."

Max and Shatina's eyes bulged, and they leapt into the shower, closing the curtain behind them just as the security officer entered the room and flipped the light on.

The man began humming the same song he'd previously been whistling - *Skip to my Lou* - as he unzipped his pants.

He took a long time releasing his bladder, then when he let out a fart, Max and Shatina glanced at each other.

"Uh oh…" he said. "It's gonna be a while."

They heard more movement like he was sitting down at the toilet, then the disgusting sounds of his bowels being released like pellets into the porcelain bowl.

Max and Shatina gagged and covered their noses with their hands as the putrid smell filled the air.

The man let out a loud grunt as he let out the last of his load, then finally grabbed the tissue to clean himself up.

Max prayed he didn't get the idea to take a quick shower while he was at it. The man flushed, but from the sounds of it, the toilet got clogged.

"Sheesh!" he said in a gruff tone, then sounds of a plunger were heard for the next few minutes. Finally he got it all down.

"Hmph, I'd better head back downstairs," he said, then he walked toward the closet. They heard him rummaging through it for a moment, then the air was filled with a much more pleasant lavender scent as he sprayed freshener.

"Much better," he said, then the room became dark again as he whistled out of the room.

Max and Shatina listened for a few more moments as his whistling grew softer, then Max swallowed. "You ready?" he whispered.

Shatina nodded, and they exited the shower, then the bathroom. Once they were back in the hallway, they listened out for sounds of any other security officers. Thankfully, there weren't any.

Lacey's room was three doors down to the left. Max and Shatina finally made it there, and it was unlocked. They entered the bedroom, closing the door behind them.

Lacey was a neat freak, judging from the freshly made bed and recently vacuumed carpets, but they were here for a job, not to inspect every inch of the room. They headed for the closet and turned on the light.

"This thing is bigger than my bedroom," Shatina remarked, as they walked inside and saw all of Lacey's clothes and shoes, coordinated by color and style.

"I bet half of these outfits have never been worn," Max remarked.

Shatina nodded in agreement, and they walked toward a full length mirror, which had several shelves of immaculately displayed jewelry sitting on it.

"God, this is like a jewelry store," Max remarked.

Shatina was all about business. "There it is," she said, pointing at the necklace.

Max looked, and indeed, the necklace was there in plain sight. He grabbed it and put it in his pocket so they could get out of Lacey's room and back to the ballroom.

They moved quietly as they exited Lacey's closet, then her bedroom. Once they were back in the hallway, they listened for more guards but didn't hear any.

Miraculously, they made it back to the kitchen to grab more bottles of wine without anyone seeing them. Max felt like they were going to get away with this, but he still felt like Lacey's necklace was burning a hole in his pocket.

As they reentered the ballroom, Max stopped short. Lacey was standing before them with a frown on her face.

He fought to maintain his composure.

"Good, finally someone who is here to do their job correctly," she snapped, then held out her glass with impatience. Max quickly refilled it.

"Good," Lacey said, then downed it, holding it out for another. Max refilled it again. She drank a few sips, then calmed. "Thank you."

Her eyes filled with tears for a moment, then she squared her shoulders. She read Max's name tag. "Nicolas, be sure to tell Augustus I said you should receive a fifteen percent bonus. You've been the best server tonight by far."

She turned to Shatina. "You two, Roxanne. Every time I've seen you two, you've been working, unlike some of these other goofballs."

She shook her head and nodded in Tyler and Malcolm's direction. They were standing with one of the guests and laughing at something he said.

"Wow, so unprofessional," Shatina said in her fake British accent. Max almost burst out laughing but kept a straight face.

Lacey walked away from them and he turned to Shatina. "You've got to stop doing that."

Chapter 29

After another half hour, Shatina felt it was time for her and Max to leave. They had refilled countless drinks, but it seemed the guests would never be satisfied. The party was still jumping, so Shatina suspected it would probably last past midnight.

"Hey, I really have to get home to my family's dinner," she said to Max the next time she caught up with him.

Max nodded. "I agree. This necklace feels like it's weighing down my pocket. The only problem is, how are we going to get out of here without being noticed?"

They were supposed to stay until the end of the party, but that was never the plan. The area where their cars were parked was behind the kitchen. It wouldn't be that hard to get there if no one noticed them, but they would need some serious luck to slip away unnoticed twice in the same night. Especially since Lacey had noticed their work.

Shatina thought for a moment. She wasn't sure how they were going to pull this off either.

As if sent by God Himself, Augustus approached them with a smile. "Nicolas, Roxanne, I was just looking for you two."

Max and Shatina shot each other nervous glances, but Augustus alleviated their fears, placing a soft hand on each of their shoulders.

"Lacey was just raving about both of you, and how you demonstrated the highest level of professionalism she had seen in a while. I must admit, I agree. Whenever we hire extra staff for an event like this, we take note of that sort of thing."

Shatina relaxed, and so did Max.

Augustus reached in his pocket and pulled out two wads of cash. "Because she was so grateful for the work you did tonight, Lacey said you two can take the night off early, and we added a fifteen percent bonus to each of your payments."

Shatina was taken aback, and from the looks of it, so was Max. She wasn't aware that they were being paid in cash.

Probably so they can report whatever amount of expenses they want to on their taxes, she thought. She imagined they paid a ton of money every year to the government, living in a place like this.

"Thank you," she and Max said in unison.

"You're sure you don't want us to finish out the night?" Max asked, and at first, Shatina was pissed at him, but then she thought about it.

"We don't mind at all," she chimed in, using her false British accent.

Augustus' eyes twinkled. "No, no, enjoy the rest of your evening. I know you two have families to get home to. Job well done, and we will likely reach out to you for future events."

"Thank you so much, sir," Max said, and Shatina shot him a huge smile as they made their way out of the ballroom. Once they were in the foyer, they walked at a brisk pace until they were outside.

Shatina acted naturally as they made their way to where the server's vehicles were parked. She was one part elated, another paranoid, and lastly guilty. She half expected one of the security officers to come running after them about the necklace.

Thankfully, they made it to Max's car without incident.

When they got inside, Shatina exhaled.

"Never again," Max said, his hand shaking as he turned his key in the ignition.

"Who are you telling?" Shatina remarked.

Chapter 30

Max's heart pounded the entire way to the cabin. This was almost over. Freedom was so close, he could almost taste it.

His heart sank, however, when they pulled up to the cabin and saw a large white envelope taped to the door.

He punched the steering wheel, causing Shatina to jump beside him. "What does she want now?" he said through clenched teeth. Sam had worked every nerve he had throughout this experience. What kind of sinister joy did she get from messing with him?

Shatina sighed, showing she was upset too. "Let's go see. Hopefully it's not anything too stupid."

"Right." They exited the vehicle and walked up to the door. Max snatched the envelope off of it and opened it up, sucking his teeth as he read the contents.

"She wants us to take the necklace to the pawn shop and bring back the receipt."

Shatina's eyes widened. "Is she serious? The diamonds in that necklace have to be registered. There's no way we make it out of a pawnshop without being handcuffed."

"Tell me about it," Max said, his sarcasm evident. He rubbed the back of his neck, which was throbbing due to the tension this situation caused him. "She left us the name and address of a location. We're supposed to meet some guy named Goldstein."

"Goldstein?" Shatina wrinkled her nose.

Max looked up the location on his phone and his heart sank yet again when he realized it was closed for the evening. "The earliest we can get there is tomorrow at seven. Let's go right when it opens so we can get this over with."

"Right," Shatina agreed. She put her hand on Max's shoulder. "It's almost over," she said.

He stared into her eyes, and the sincerity he saw almost brought a tear to his eyes. "Right. Thank God. After this, I'm on the straight and narrow for good."

"Tell me about it," she said.

Max dropped Shatina back off at her apartment. "Hey," she said, turning back after she got out. Max slid down the window to hear her more clearly.

"I just thought of something...what are you doing tonight?"

He shrugged, and it looked like she felt bad.

"I would ask you to come to my parent's house, but..."

Max waved her off to let her it was okay. "I get it. They don't know we're associated with each other."

Shatina nodded. "I'll bring you a plate, okay?"

That warmed his heart. "Thanks. I would definitely appreciate that."

She smiled, then waved before heading inside. Max drove off to his apartment, prepared to eat a TV dinner and watch the game.

***

The next morning, Max showed up bright and early to pick Shatina up, and she was ready with a container in hand that felt like it was filled with food. Max's hand was weighed down when she handed it to him.

"Dang, 'Tina!" he said. "You came through."

Shatina smiled, then opened her mouth to say something, but closed it.

"What?" Max said.

She shook her head, then brushed a strand of hair behind her ear. "Nothing, it's just that you called me 'Tina. I haven't heard you say that in a while."

Max's smile faltered. "Oh, my bad. I didn't mean to bring back memories…"

She stopped him. "No, you're good. It's just…I kind of like it."

They stared at each other for a few moments, Max's heart pounding a mile a minute. He wanted to lean over and kiss her but didn't want to ruin the moment.

"We better go," he said softly instead, and Shatina nodded.

They made it to the pawn shop. When they pulled up outside, Max turned to Shatina. "I'll go in so you won't be shown on the cameras, but I wanted to tell you something first."

Shatina searched his eyes. "What is it?"

Max pulled out the necklace and locket, which he had separated.

She gasped. "It's broken?"

Max shook his head. "No, it's not broken, but I took a peek inside." He opened the locket so Shatina could see.

There was a picture of a younger Lacey with her father. Once Max opened the locket the night prior, he did some digging online and found out that the man had died in a fire. The picture obviously held sentimental value, which was probably why Sam picked this particular necklace.

"Gotcha," Shatina said, like she was catching his drift.

"I'm sending the locket back to Lacey," he said as more of a statement than a question.

Shatina nodded. "Sam is a little too power hungry for her own good anyway. How will she ever find out?"

Max nodded, then went inside.

Thankfully, Goldstein immediately recognized him. "Sam sent you?" he asked.

Max nodded at the older man with an eyebrow ring and tattoos up both arms.

"What you got for me?" Goldstein asked.

Max handed him the necklace.

Goldstein's eyes widened as he let out a whistle. "Wow, now that's a beauty. Likely worth thousands."

Max stood silent, waiting to finish the transaction. Goldstein carried the necklace to the back, then came back to face Max, opening the cash register and pulling out some money, then printing out a receipt. "Thank you for your business," he said.

Max counted the cash. "Only five hundred bucks?"

Goldstein shrugged. "That was the amount Sam and I agreed upon. What's it to you?" The man sounded defensive, so Max took that as his cue to leave.

"Thanks," he said, and exited the shop without another word.

Chapter 31

Now that the drama with Sam was over, Shatina only had her Dark Psychology class to trouble her. She already received failing grades on two out of the three assigned papers for the course, so if she didn't pass this last paper, it was over.

Ted hadn't bothered her after she confronted him outside class that night, but she could only imagine what he was going to do when he saw her twenty page paper on white collar crime and the personality types who flocked to it.

"I swear, he better not pull any stunts with this one," Shatina said. She had gone above and beyond and reached out to the author of one of the research articles she used for the paper and interviewed her for her perspective. The author shared extensive insights, which Shatina was extremely grateful for.

She only hoped Ted would see her hard work the same way.

The semester was ending, and it was the last day of classes. Since this paper was her last assignment for Dark Psychology and her other finals were held during the last week of classes, Shatina didn't have to return to campus for finals week.

She was grateful for that, because it meant that today was the last time she had to see this school until winter break was over.

The month-long vacation was much awaited, especially with everything else that had been going on.

At Thanksgiving dinner, Shatina's father announced that they were headed to California for winter vacation, and Shatina couldn't be more excited. Two weeks out of state would do her good.

She smiled as she thought of Max. She wondered how he was feeling now that Sam was out of their hair?

Shatina didn't have much time to dwell on that thought process, because Ted entered the amphitheater, fashionably late as usual.

He was carrying a stack of papers with him, which Shatina presumed to be their final assignments.

Anticipation could be felt throughout the room. Shatina wanted nothing more than to get her grade so she could know where she stood.

Ted pointed at one of the women in the front row, but before he could tell her to pass out the papers, a male student raised his hand.

"Chester?" Ted addressed him.

"Ted, I had a question."

Ted nodded. "Go on."

"Why do you only ask the female students to pass out the papers and handouts?"

A pin drop could be heard in the room after Chester finished his question.

Ted stared at him for a long time before his face broke out in a huge smile. "Finally. I thought no one would ever ask. Everybody, give Chester a round of applause."

Nervous applause sounded around the room, but Ted gestured for them to go harder. "Come on, you can do better than that!" The applause immediately grew louder. When it died down, Ted smiled again. "Chester, you are the first student in three semesters who had the decency to confront me about this peculiarity in my behavior. What made you do it?"

Chester stammered as if he was unsure what to say. "Well...I just noticed...it's unfair."

Ted nodded in agreement. "You're absolutely right, it was unfair. Sometimes it takes a person like you to stand up for the rights of others, while everyone else just sits there and watches."

The room grew silent again as everyone contemplated the weight of Ted's words. Shatina agreed with him, she had wished for years that someone would stand up for her before she began taking matters into her own hands, but Ted's show of decency didn't make her like him any more.

Ted presented the stack of papers to Chester, which were likely face down with the student's name on the back, like the others had been. "Would you do the honors?"

Chester nodded and took the papers, carefully passing them around to his classmates. One by one, Shatina watched her classmates receive their papers, but her heart sank once Chester got to the last paper and she didn't receive one.

She had been busy watching Chester like a hawk, but now that he was done, she focused on Ted, who was studying her.

She fought the urge to roll her eyes. What did he want now?

Ted said they were done for the semester, so everyone began filing out, many students thanking him for a great semester as they exited the amphitheater.

Hence his controversial reviews, Shatina thought with a glare in his direction.

She waited until the last student was gone before she approached him.

"Ted? I didn't receive my paper."

"I know," he said, then produced it from his back pocket. Shatina hadn't noticed it sticking out because Ted had stood facing the class for the entire period.

She reached out for it, quickly opening the fold to see her grade. Unlike the other papers, there was no grade at the top.

"What is it?" she said, searching Ted's eyes for answers. "Where's my grade?"

Ted swallowed. "Truthfully, it could either be an A or an F. That all depends on you."

Shatina was confused. "What do you mean? I made sure to follow the rubric. I even went above and beyond. What was missing?"

Ted continued to stare at her. "I will award you with an A on your paper, and for the class. But I need you to agree to something."

"Agree to what?" Shatina was becoming flustered, she was so pissed. She wanted this whole situation to be over already.

"I need your help with something," Ted replied, as if he didn't notice the tension in her features. "Can I count on you to keep your word?"

Chapter 32

Sam studied Lacey's social media page for days after the Thanksgiving gala. After almost a week, she finally found what she was looking for.

Lacey did a live video, crying her eyes out about how she had misplaced her locket. "I swore I put my necklace back in the same place I always do, but it came up missing!" She let out a few more tears before speaking again. "That necklace held a locket containing a picture of my father. I don't know what to do, it was the last thing I had from him!" With that statement, she let out a loud wail that could warm the coldest of hearts.

Sam cackled, then rewound the video so she could see that moment again before exiting out of the app.

"Mission accomplished," she said, stretching and yawning. Now that that situation was over, maybe she should answer one of Brighton's incessant calls to tell him to piss off. He got himself into the situation he was in, it was his job to get out of it.

Once he was out, they could discuss the possibility of a relationship.

Sam had been toying with the idea of rekindling something with Max, but he didn't seem to be interested.

He was all googly eyed over Shatina, who Sam had to admit had earned her respect.

"This is a cause for celebration!" Sam said, clapping her hands, then grabbing her burner cell from her nightstand to send Max and Shatina one final text message.

Her face broke out into a wide grin as they both texted her back, complaining that they thought they were done with her now that the deal was done.

She didn't bother to text back, but she knew they would show up to their final meeting with the footage still looming over their heads.

***

Friday night came, and Sam was oozing with excitement as she carried the bottle of Chardonnay, along with a brand new pack of wine glasses, into the cabin. She had told Max and Shatina to be there at seven, but she showed up after eight, just to add to the suspense. She knew they both had to be on the edge of their seats, wondering what scheme she had cooked up now.

As she suspected, Sam was met with angry looks from both of them.

She strode up to the table and placed the bottle down first, then opened up the bag to take out the box of glasses.

"What is this?" Max asked.

Sam pursed her lips. "I thought we would have a little party. If we get too tipsy, we can spend the night here and leave out in the morning."

"I'm not drinking with you," Shatina said. "Our deal is done, Sam. Let's not prolong this any further." She stood to leave.

"Wow, Shatina, that hurt my feelings," Sam said with a pout. "I thought we were building a bond with all the time we've spent together."

"You need to see a therapist if a bond is what you thought we were building," Max said, and that comment actually did hurt Sam's feelings. She refused to show it though.

"Very well," she said, holding back her emotions. "I'll drink myself, but you two at least have to listen to my speech first."

They were silent for a moment, then Max sighed, while Shatina rolled her eyes and sat back down.

"Please make this quick," Shatina said.

Sam opened the bottle, then poured some in three glasses, sliding one each to Max and Shatina, despite their prior protests. Perhaps they would loosen up after they realized she was letting them go for good after tonight.

She drank her glass slowly, while Shatina and Max watched with pained expressions on their faces, neither of them touching their glasses.

Once she finished, Sam poured another glass.

Shatina drew out an exasperated breath, and Max wiped his hand down his face, but neither of them said anything.

Sam decided to stop toying with them. She put her glass back down onto the table.

"Okay." She straightened up in her seat, feeling a little woozy. She never was much of a drinker. "I wanted to thank you both for a job well done. You played it exactly as we discussed, and Lacey got what she deserved."

She didn't say anything after that, but Max and Shatina stared as if they expected her to continue.

She reached for her glass again. "You can go. I'll see you around."

"And the footage?" Max asked.

"Already deleted," Sam said, which was a lie, but she would get around to it eventually.

"We're done for good?" Shatina asked with hesitation in her tone.

"Yup, now go on, before I think of something else."

Max and Shatina hastily rose from their seats, but everyone in the room froze as a male voice sounded from one of the back rooms.

"Wait a second, that can't be it!" He sounded amused, and Sam recognized his voice before he emerged from the shadows. She was staring at her contact, who was wearing a sinister smile eerily similar to the one she wore when dealing with Max and Shatina during their prior interactions.

Shatina sputtered as she spoke. "Buster? What the hell are you doing here?"

Max looked confused, before he put two and two together himself. "Buster?" he said to Shatina. "From your notebook?"

Buster chuckled, then took a bow. "Live in the flesh," he said.

Shatina looked utterly defeated. "What do you want?" she asked.

Buster glanced at Sam, then focused back on Shatina. "Shatina...long time, no see. Bet you never thought we would cross paths again."

Shatina looked at Sam like she couldn't believe what was happening. "This whole time, you two were working together?"

Buster nodded and cut in before Sam could answer. "Yup, she sure was. Don't worry, Shatina. This will be painless. You may have gotten away with what you did to me all those years ago, but it's time to reap what you have sown."

Chapter 33

This was ridiculous. Max thought he and Shatina were scot-free, and they were, but only for a moment. Now Shatina was all wrapped up again, and this time it was still Max's fault. If he hadn't uploaded that copy of her notebook to his cloud, Sam never would have found it when she hacked it.

"How did you two meet, anyway?" Max asked after Buster's identity was revealed.

Sam cut in. "We dated briefly. Purely out of coincidence." She gave Buster an indiscernible look after that.

"Coincidence, my left foot!" Buster said with a chuckle. "Come on Sam, you targeted me. Admit it."

Sam didn't respond. Gone was her smug expression, however. Max assumed that meant she hadn't seen this coming.

Maybe that's a good thing, he thought. *If Sam is against Buster overstepping his position, maybe Shatina and I can work with her to get rid of him.*

Max pondered it for a moment, then Shatina spoke up.

"Buster, what do you want from me? I'm sorry for messing with your car, okay? In my defense, you stood me up after stringing me along, making me think you were into me."

"Wrong," Buster said. "If you would have had the decency to wait til the next day, I would have been able to explain to you that I was out with my cousin Michael, his girlfriend, and his girlfriend's sister. He called me last minute begging me to go so the sister wouldn't be a third wheel. I was going to make it up to you."

Shatina fell silent, but Buster continued.

"Anyway, that's water under the bridge. That little incident was nothing, I've been over that."

"Why are you here then?" Shatina asked. "Why are you holding it over my head, talking about it's time for me to reap what I've sown?"

Buster flipped his hand to wave off her question. "That was a joke. I do need you to do something for me, but not for revenge. It's mainly because I can't do it myself, and...you do owe me one."

Shatina rolled her eyes. "What is it, Buster?"

Buster's stance shifted. "I'll fill you in on the details later." He reached in his back pocket and pulled out two burner phones, tossing one to Shatina and the other to Max.

"Sorry, Sam," he said, focusing on her for the first time since the conversation began.

Since he had said his piece, Buster saw fit to leave the cabin.

Max, Sam, and Shatina watched as Buster walked into the woods until he disappeared.

"How long was he back there?" Sam asked, as if she had just snapped out of a trance.

"It doesn't matter!" Shatina snapped. "This is all your fault. We did everything you told us to, but you had to dig up some guy from my past to be your contact? What's wrong with you?"

Sam looked as if she was about to offer Shatina an apology, but she stopped herself, her expression hardened. "No, it's not my fault." She crossed her arms. "Your silly teenage self left a fully detailed account of what happened, names and all. The evidence was right there for someone to find it. And all because some boy stood you up? You're pathetic."

"You're the one who's pathetic!" Shatina bellowed, looking like she was ready to fight. "You tried to force me to compete with you over Max, all because you were insecure. You dangled that footage over our head for months, all because of some silly game. Don't you realize that our entire lives could be destroyed over something we didn't do if we get outed to the police?"

The two women were at each other's throats now. Sam clapped back at Shatina's statement. "Don't you realize that if you and Max's plan had worked that night, I wouldn't even be breathing?"

The tension in the room was thick as a knife for what felt like an eternity.

Max felt like he should say something, but he was at a loss for words.

Shatina gave in first. "Look Sam, I never got a chance to tell you this, but I'm sorry. I take full responsibility for my actions that night."

Max studied Sam. Depending on how she responded, they might be able to work together to take Buster down after all.

"Thank you for your apology," Sam huffed, but offered nothing more. Instead, she whirled around and exited the cabin, stalking over to her jeep and peeling off like she always did.

Shatina stared at Max. "What have I gotten myself into now?"

***

As if the day wasn't long enough, after Max dropped Shatina off at her apartment, he went home to find his brother Jared posted up outside of his, smoking a cigarette.

"What are you doing here?" Max asked, and that was when he caught sight of the three teardrop tattoos that trailed below Jared's left eye.

He had heard rumors about those types of tattoos being gang related and symbolizing how many bodies a person dropped, but he wasn't about to question Jared about it now.

Jared cracked a smile, then flicked his cigarette to the ground and stomped it out.

"What? No hey baby bro, glad you got out early?"

Max sighed. "Look, Jared. I would have let you stay with me, but I got a lot going on."

"I know what you got going on," Jared said, matter of factly.

Max drew a blank. What was he talking about? There was no way he could possibly know.

"I'm saying though," Jared continued. "Now that I'm out, how about you cut me in?"

Max calmed. Jared was talking about the pills, not the Sam situation. "Look bro, I would do that, but I'm out of the game."

He attempted to say his words with the same amount of swag that flowed effortlessly from Jared's lips, but it

135

came out sounding like Max was a glorified nerd who was just learning street lingo.

Jared smirked. "Get back in."

Max rubbed the back of his neck, feeling cornered by the hardened look on Jared's face. He had no idea what his brother would do to him if he denied his request. He took another route.

"What if you get caught? I'm pretty sure that's a violation of your parole."

Jared shrugged, then smirked again like he had already thought about that. "See Max? You were always the smart one, like I told you while we were growing up. You won't have to worry about me, because my hands won't get dirty in this situation."

He stared at Max, until Max put two and two together to realize what he was saying.

"You're going to have me sell the drugs and give you the money," he said in a dry tone.

Jared's smile was genuine this time. "We'll be more like partners, except you do the leg work. I'll even give you a percentage. How does sixty-forty sound? I figure that's only fair, since we are brothers and all."

Chapter 34

Sam was beyond pissed at Buster. How dare he think he could bust up in her cabin calling shots like he was the boss? She was the head of this operation, not him.

Still, he had access to all the evidence that Sam had eagerly supplied him, back when she was excited about getting back at Shatina and Max.

Now Sam regretted that decision, though she wouldn't be admitting it any time soon. Buster had to be stopped, and he would be, it was only a matter of time.

All Sam had to do was find out some dirt on him that was bigger than whatever he wanted Max and Shatina to do, and presto! He would be gone.

She wasn't concerned about doing Max and Shatina any favors, despite what they had done for her with Lacey. It was the principle of the thing for her. Buster, and men in general, seemed to think they could do whatever they wanted, whenever they wanted, without any consequences.

Brighton was like that, and so was Buster, and so was her father. It was time for all of them to learn their lessons, even if Sam had to teach them individually.

Brighton had stopped blowing up her phone after he got the picture. McConnell's calls ceased too. Sam figured that must have meant he found another angle.

"Hm, let's see what he comes up with," she remarked.

Sam's mind traveled to Lacey again, the one part of her life that was going well at the moment. She decided to get drunk, watch Lacey's live video again and laugh herself to oblivion.

Sam ran to the kitchen to grab a bottle of wine, then returned to her bedroom, hooking her phone up to the 76" TV so she could watch on the big screen.

She would likely only have a glass before she started feeling tipsy, but that was fine with her. Once the phone's screen was displayed on her TV, Sam typed in Lacey's name on the social media app, clicked on her page, then scrolled down.

She was holding her wine glass in her other hand and almost dropped it on her bed when she saw a new photo with Lacey wearing a necklace identical to the first, with the locket hanging from it.

Sam's pupils pored over every word in the caption Lacey provided.

Look what an anonymous angel sent me! I got back my locket. Plus, my boyfriend had insurance on the necklace, so I was able to get a new one. Good vibes only this weekend. About to head out for a night on the town.

Sam was so furious she threw her phone at the TV and slammed her wine glass down on the nightstand.

She missed the TV by a few inches, and some of the wine splashed over onto the wooden stand and her carpeted floor, but Sam could hardly think straight.

Boyfriend? Dexter and Lacey were official? How dare he? *That pig…*

Sam realized at that moment why she hadn't heard from her father in a while. He had given up and decided to pursue his relationship with Lacey full force.

Sam imagined them spending the night together, laughing about how the incident had given them a scare, but how it worked out for their good.

Sam saw red.

She barely realized that her phone had clicked out of streaming mode so her regular TV was playing one of the news channels.

Her ears perked up at the mention of breaking news about Brighton Miller.

Sam's jaw dropped when the newscaster said that Brighton had waived his right to trial.

"What?" Sam bugged out. "Why would he do that?" She racked her brains for answers but came up short. Sam had no idea why Brighton would give up on a chance to sway a jury with his charming looks and otherwise impeccable record.

Sam's heart sank as the weight of the situation hit her. Brighton was going down. The only man who ever said he loved her was about to be convicted of murder.

Not if she could help it.

Sam knew it was messed up, but Max and Shatina shouldn't have crossed her. She hurried to her laptop before she could change her mind, found the video file she was looking for, and sent it to the chief of police.

Chapter 35

Shatina's mind was swimming with the recent turn of events. Ted wanted something from her, and she had to help him or he would turn her grade of *Incomplete* into an *F*, Buster had her backed against the wall, and Max had texted her last night, telling her that his brother was forcing him back into the drug game.

She could never catch a break.

Every time she got to a point where she thought her problems were over, here came something else. Was she *reaping what she had sowed*, as Buster suggested? She couldn't get those words out of her mind since he had spoken them.

Buster said he was over what she had done to his car, but he was still blackmailing her about it. And to think, if he was telling her the truth about him not standing her up all those years ago, she'd gone after him for no reason.

Shatina felt like the scum of the earth.

Her family vacation couldn't have come at a better time. If Shatina had it her way, she would disappear in California and stay there.

She shook her head. No, she couldn't do that. Buster was probably tracking her every move, like Sam had.

Out of the frying pan and into the fire, the voice said. *Maybe you can jump into the ocean.*

Shatina snorted. "Hello to you too."

She hadn't heard the voice in a while, but she imagined it would be coming on more frequently now that she was under so much pressure.

She had no one in the world to turn to except Max, and, to a degree, her sister Shatara.

For the second time since this fiasco began, Shatina wondered if she should go to the police and turn herself in. As Ted remarked, it was possible she could wriggle her way into a lenient sentence if she went before a jury. She had done it before, why not again?

"No, I can't leave Max hanging," she said, shaking her head.

It was strangely ironic that a twisted turn of fate had led her and Max into working together for the fourth time.

"Maybe this time will actually be the last time," Shatina said with another roll of her eyes, before she grabbed her luggage to roll it out to her father's waiting minivan.

***

The flight went smoothly, which Shatina took as a sign that this vacation would bring the peace she needed.

Her parents had rented out a hotel suite for themselves, then another for Shatina, Shatara, Tyonne, and Tamika.

Shatina found herself getting excited at the prospect of pretending to be normal again, even if it was only for a couple of weeks.

They spent the night at the hotel, ordering room service and chatting the night away, then the next morning they headed to Universal Studios.

Shatina let her hair down and had a blast, reasoning that this was probably the last time she would get to do this for a while.

Halfway through the day, she told Shatara, Tyonne, and Tamika to go ahead of her and stand in the long line for the next ride they planned to go on, while she scooted away to the bathroom.

"You sure you don't want one of us to go with you?" Shatara asked, but Shatina shook her head.

"No sis, I'm good. Just hold my place and I'll make sure to hurry."

"Cool."

Shatina raced off and used the bathroom, then bounded out of the stall to wash her hands so she could hurry back to the ride as promised.

She was so focused on trying to scan the line to see where her sister, cousin, and best friend were standing that she bumped into a solid, muscular man and fell back onto her butt.

"Oh no, I'm so sorry," he said, and reached out to help her up.

Then they both froze.

Shatina, because she was staring into the eyes of a ghost, and Seth, because he thought he would never again cross paths with the love of his life.

Before you go...

Dear Reader,

Please don't hate me! Lol. The plot thickens with this ending, which will undoubtedly leave some on the edge of their seats. Have no fear, the next installment is at your fingertips. Check out book four in the Quiet Ones series, <u>Reap What You Sow</u>, to see what happens next.

Until next time,

Tanisha Stewart

PS: If you loved this story, please go ahead and leave a rating or review! No spoilers, please. I would love to hear from you!

Tanisha Stewart's Books

Even Me Series
Even Me
Even Me, The Sequel
Even Me, Full Circle

When Things Go Series
When Things Go Left
When Things Get Real
When Things Go Right

For My Good Series
For My Good: The Prequel
For My Good: My Baby Daddy Ain't Ish
For My Good: I Waited, He Cheated
For My Good: Torn Between The Two
For My Good: You Broke My Trust
For My Good: Better or Worse
For My Good: Love and Respect
Rick and Sharmeka: A BWWM Romance

Betrayed Series
Betrayed By My So-Called Friend
Betrayed By My So-Called Friend, Part 2
Betrayed 3: Camaiyah's Redemption
Betrayed Series: Special Edition

Phate Series
Phate: An Enemies to Lovers Romance
Phate 2: An Enemies to Lovers Romance
Leisha & Manuel: Love After Pain

The Real Ones Series
Find You A Real One: A Friends to Lovers Romance
Find You A Real One 2: A Friends to Lovers Romance
Janie & E: Life Lessons

The Quiet Ones Series
Should Have Thought Twice: A Psychological Thriller
Fooled Me Once: A Psychological Thriller
Never Saw Me Coming: A Psychological Thriller
Reap What You Sow: A Psychological Thriller
Surprise Surprise: A Psychological Thriller
The Enemy You Know: A Psychological Thriller

Standalones
A Husband, A Boyfriend, & a Side Dude
In Love With My Uber Driver
You Left Me At The Altar
Where. Is. Haseem?! A Romantic-Suspense Comedy
Caught Up With The 'Rona: An Urban Sci-Fi Thriller
#DOLO: An Awkward, Non-Romantic Journey Through Singlehood
December 21st: An Urban Supernatural Suspense
Everybody Ain't Your Friend
The Maintenance Man
Not What It Seems